Seasons of the Wild
a wildlife center mystery

by

Jacqueline A. Carl

Seasons of the Wild: A Wildlife Center Mystery

Copyright © 2015 by JAJACquest

This is a work of fiction. Names, characters, places, and incidents are either the product of the author's imagination or are used fictitiously. Any resemblance to actual persons, living or dead, events, or locations is entirely coincidental.

All rights reserved. No part of this book may be used or reproduced in any manner whatsoever without written permission except in the case of brief quotations embodied in critical articles or reviews. For information address: JAJACquest, P.O. Box 1246, Molalla OR 97038

ISBN: 978-0-9892229-6-9

Printed in the United States of America

JAJACquest paperback edition / June 2015

All rights reserved.

Table of Contents

Prologue

Winter Dreams..1

Sparks that Inspire 23

Spring Break-In 41

May Day Masquerade..65

Summer Wishes 85

Autumn Reaping 119

Giving Thanks..129

All Hallows Eve..143

Prologue

Oh my God, I can't believe I actually stole it. Now what? I swallowed hard. My throat was dry and I could feel my heart pounding in my ears. I shivered at the cold sweat covered my body, but tried to act natural as I scanned the room with forced casualness. I don't think anyone noticed me swiping and wrapping it loosely in my jacket, but I knew that wouldn't last long. *I have to figure out how to get it out of here. And soon.*

A short distance away, Paige, Meagan, and Kensi laughed. *They'd flirt with any guy who strolled by,* I scoffed. *What a bunch of snobs. They're so caught up in their own petty lives they wouldn't notice a thing unless it jumped up and bit them.* But I knew not everyone was so preoccupied, or wouldn't be for very long.

Hssss. Across the room a red headed vulture cursed and flapped large wings at a dog that passed too close to the wildlife center's information table. *Clank. Clatter.* The leash that held the bird to its stand perch rattled as it jumped away from the offending terrier. The commotion caught the attention of the entire room, including the kids at my booth.

Now's my chance. "Going to the bathroom." I murmured to no one in particular. I hoped nobody would wonder why I was taking my jacket to the restroom. Snaking through the crowd, I escaped the auditorium and headed for the vestry.

Backpacks lay stuffed under the benches that lined one wall of the entrance hall. I stared in horror at the open front door. Mama was just outside, greeting people as they came in. *Now what? If she sees me, I'm toast. I can't sneak it outta here with her standing there. And, if anyone notices it's missing, I'll be the first one they suspect.*

A quick thought. I headed for the backpacks, plopped down and hunted for mine. *Not this one, nor that one.* I tossed one after another aside searching. *Why did Mama and I have to be one of the first ones here?* My big blue bag was buried.

Rattled, I was beginning to find it hard to think. I grit my teeth to keep my hands from shaking. *Where is it?* My mind screamed. When I finally found the bag, I stuffed the box inside, hiding it in a bunch of dirty gym clothes. *There.* I glanced around to see if I'd been noticed but, so far, the coast was clear. *With any luck I'll walk it right outta here and no one will be the wiser.* I zipped up the pack and hurried back to the main room.

Winter Dreams

Hissssss. The turkey vulture fluffed his feathers and spread his wings, trying to make himself look bigger, fiercer. He rattled the tether tying him to his standing perch, drawing the attention of most of people in the room. The offending terrier jumped a few inches back and responded with a low growl.

Splat. Cyrano defecated onto the papers spread under his perch laid there to protect the carpeted floor of the church meeting hall. A strong, acrid smell began its slow trip around the room.

Ewww. The four-year-old girl standing opposite their small display table grabbed her nose; a disgusted expression filled her face. "Why did he do that?"

"The dog scared him," Morgan answered matter-of-factly. Having sat at information booths with her mother, a wildlife veterinarian, since she was a baby, 13-year old Morgan knew everything about the animals, and their nonprofit rehabilitation center.

"Could be worse," Morgan's best friend Lawren piped in. Helping Morgan keep an eye on the animals at the information booth, she handed a flier to another passer-by. "At least he didn't barf," she giggled, referring to the vulture's nasty habit of regurgitating food when stressed.

And if you think, it smells bad going down . . . Morgan kept the scent memory to herself. *No point in totally grossing everyone out.*

The little girl and the dog on the over-long leash were dragged away by a woman who looked to be on a mission. Cyrano started to preen his feathers back into place. Morgan collected the soiled newspaper and stuffed it into a sealed plastic garbage can before people would complain about the smell.

"I'm getting hungry." Lawren tucked her light brown hair behind her ear.

"Mom and Aunt Jackie should be back from their break soon." Morgan scanned the busy room. Identical twins, both her mom and aunt were tall and had the same light blonde hair as Morgan. They were usually easy to spot in a crowd.

A few booths down some kids about her age were decorating the church's Christmas tree, laughing and chatting while they worked. *Looks like fun,* Morgan sighed. More fun than being stuck listening to other people's long-winded animal stories, or fielding their pest problems.

The glint of an unusually bright flash reflecting from the tree's topper caught Morgan's eye. A photographer from the local newspaper snapped shots of the kids and tree. Several of the girls mugged for the camera, holding the fancy ornament in its box between them. A dark haired boy she didn't recognize ducked behind the tree to avoid being photographed.

Morgan blinked her eyes a few times, waiting for the lingering white floater in her vision to go away. Her stomach growled. "What's there to eat here?" she asked Lawren.

"The usual." Lawren nodded toward the room's small kitchen. Pancakes and donuts, spaghetti and soup, cookies and cupcakes, all sat on diner-style linoleum counter waiting to be purchased by hungry patrons. "Whatever the Bazaar committee could scrounge up."

"Or make easy and cheap," said Morgan.

Click. Another cell phone took a picture of Cyrano. The buzzard's bald, red head flushed. He looked very pleased with himself.

* * * * *

Morgan shivered against the icy gust of wind that pushed its way through the opening front door of the wildlife sanctuary. Seated on the reception room couch, she looked up from the book she was reading to see who had come in.

"Hi, Morgan." Pastor Michaels pulled off her rain-soaked cap and gloves. Beside her stood a sulky boy who looked like he was doing his best not to see Morgan. *Hey, that's the guy from the Holiday Craft Bazaar, the one that ducked behind the Christmas tree.*

Morgan greeted the portly Lutheran minister, wondering what had brought her to their wildlife care clinic. She studied the disheveled boy standing next to her. He looked scrawny beside the large woman in the imposing black garb and white clerical collar.

"Good to see you, Pastor." Morgan's mom extended her hand in greeting. "This must be Lucan." The veterinarian smiled at the boy, who only gave her a quick glance before lowering his eyes.

Pastor Michaels swiped the boy's knit cap off his head from behind, revealing a mass of dark, wavy hair. "Hello Dr. Ackermann." She turned to Lucan and explained. "Dr. Ackermann is the veterinarian here at the American Wildlife Foundation. She and her sister run the refuge."

Morgan scrutinized him, wondering. *I think I know him. Well, sort of. He's in my homeroom at school. He might even be in a couple of my classes.* It was hard to remember; the guy was a ghost, always sitting in the back of the room.

Lucan shoved a rebellious forelock out of his face and folded his arms across his chest.

Most of the kids in Morgan's school had been born in the small town of Molalla. She'd known them since the first grade. Lucan had only joined her class at the beginning of the school term. Morgan hadn't paid much attention to him since he seemed intentionally stand-offish, keeping to himself even at recess.

"Lucan would like to fulfill his community service hours at the wildlife center this winter."

Mandatory high school community service hours weren't usually assigned until junior or senior year, Morgan knew. *Unless you've done something wrong.* She wondered what had earned the boy additional time.

Dr. Ackermann threw her daughter *the look* as she took the form from the pastor.

Morgan sighed disappointedly, but took the hint. She got up and went into the adjoining treatment room to give them some privacy. Not that there was any real privacy in the small manufactured home that served as the wildlife center's animal care clinic. The walls were thin and the main rooms had an open floor-plan. She could still hear everything without trying, so it wasn't really eavesdropping.

"Is that true?" she heard her mother ask. Mom had no use for reluctant volunteers.

Morgan imagined Lucan shrugging his shoulders before he finally answered. "I guess."

"Lucan's been acting out," said the pastor. "And he's fallen behind in school because his family has had to relocate several times. I was hoping Morgan might tutor him."

Morgan sighed. *More work.* Acting out could mean anything from mouthing off to petty vandalism and even theft. Lawren's father was an attorney and, at his wife's request, had intervened on behalf of a troubled kid on more than one occasion. Morgan wondered what Lucan had done.

She heard her mother walk to the file cabinet and pull out one of the creaky metal drawers. It slammed shut. "I'll need you to fill out this form, and have your parents sign it. That is, if you decide you want to work here."

"*If?*" His tone was sour. "I have a choice?"

"You don't have a choice to do community service hours," Mom told him. "But you can choose to fulfill your requirements somewhere else. You may not want to work here after you learn what the ground rules are."

"Ground rules?"

"I'm inclined to let people find their own way," she said, "but you can only do that if you come here with the right attitude."

"*Any* bad behavior and you'll be sent home immediately." Morgan had never heard Pastor Michaels speak so crossly before. "Understand?"

Silence, except for the squeaking of a fidgeting wet tennis shoe.

"Once we decide on your schedule," the wildlife center manager continued, "I expect you to be here on time and for the full shift. Make sure you've eaten and you're dressed properly. We've got protective gear here, gloves, goggles, and the like, but you'll need appropriate footwear, preferably boots."

"Will I be working with the animals?"

"Sort of. You'll be cleaning pens and feeding them," Mom told him, "but this isn't a shelter for pets. Wildlife considers you a predator," she said matter-of-factly. "They don't want to be petted, and you need to be careful. I don't want any of them hurt by ramming into pen walls trying to get away from you."

Apparently, that stirred his curiosity. "What kind of animals?" he questioned.

"Glad you asked." She heard her mother grab a coat off the rack. "I'll give you a quick tour while we go over the rest of the rules. Sleep on it and let me know if you still want to do your community service hours here. You'll have to ask Morgan if she will tutor you."

Morgan was aghast when she heard the door shut. *I'll tutor him, but don't want to work with someone from my class*, she thought. Particularly not *him*. Cleaning and feeding animals at a wildlife center is dirty and hard, and not at all as glamorous as it might seem. And unlike pets, which can purr, lick your hand, or wag their tail, wildlife is decidedly unappreciative.

That night Morgan rushed through her bedtime blessing pretty much by rote. She lay awake in her room for a long time. Even her cat Willow, who's rumbling purr had lulled her to sleep since she was a baby, couldn't still her thoughts.

Don't I have a say in this? The wildlife center is my *place. Why can't he do his community service at the church? What'll my friends think? What if he's a criminal? We have drugs at the clinic. What if he steals something? Well, I guess that's not likely,* she had to admit, *considering most everything is kept under lock and key. Still, what if he hurts any of the animals? They're my friends. Does he even like animals?*

It was a while before she finally fell into a fitful sleep, haunted by her own wild imaginings.

* * * * *

Tick. Tick. Tick. The clock slowly counted the seconds. During winter break a few short weeks later Morgan found herself sitting across from Lucan in the reception room at the wildlife center helping him with his schoolwork. It was snowing outside. *Flip.* Lucan turned the page of his book. Although he had fallen behind, he was quickly catching up with school work, and with only minimal tutoring from her.

He's not slow, thought Morgan as she moved to the couch for a break. She sat, crossing her legs and closing her eyes. Her imagination magnified every sound.

Lucan plopped his pencil onto his book, and she heard his chair creak as he pushed himself hard into the backrest. "What are you doing?" he asked.

"I meditate every day." Morgan squeezed her eyes shut, forcing herself to concentrate. "Well, I *try* to." Her annoyance blamed him for distracting her. Lucan was at the wildlife center after school three days a week, and that was three days a week too often as far as she was concerned.

"That's just weird," said Lucan.

"No, it's not," she insisted. "It helps me focus."

"Focus on what?"

Morgan expelled her breath loudly and opened her eyes, her concentration blown. "I don't know. On whatever I need to, I guess." She wanted to hold him responsible for her inability to achieve the desired mental state, but she knew it wasn't entirely his fault. Learning to quiet her mind was proving to be tougher than she'd anticipated. "Aunt Jackie says you can do anything, once you learn to control your mind." It seemed simple enough, but Morgan found herself having trouble even sitting still for more than ten minutes at a time. And the events of her life rattled around in her brain like a noisy freight train.

She thought of her friends, most of which were gone during winter break. Even Lawren was spending the holidays visiting grandparents with her family.

Morgan got up and walked to their Christmas tree which, until that morning, had stood bare in a corner of the small reception room. Keeping her back to Lucan, she fiddled with an ornament—a large, spider sitting on a glittering frozen web. She moved it from branch to branch until she found a spot where it could hang freely. Inhaling deeply, she enjoyed how the smell of the fresh cut noble fir filled the room.

"What's with the spider?" Lucan balanced on the back two legs of his chair. "It's not Halloween."

"Don't you know the story of the poor woman who couldn't afford Christmas?" Morgan dropped her eyes; her tone had been sharper than she'd meant. She recited the story from memory, having heard every year during the holidays for most of her life.

"There once was a selfless woman who was kind to everyone, including the animals." Morgan smiled softly; many of the stories she knew involved animals. "One year, when things were particularly hard, the woman found she couldn't afford any gifts for her family. Not even decorations for the tree."

Morgan could feel Lucan's clear blue eyes watching her. It sent a tiny shiver curiously up her spine. "On Yule, the longest night of the year, the animals decided to decorate her family's tree to thank her for all her kindness. While the animals hung nuts, colored bits of string, and anything else they could find, the spiders spun long webs from branch to branch."

Morgan squirmed, suddenly self-conscious. *I bet he thinks my story is childish.* She forced herself to finish. "When they were done, Mother Nature sent the mist, and soon drops of dew hung from the thin strands. In one arctic breath Jack Frost froze the droplets, making ice crystals that sparkled in the moonlight like diamonds." She hastened the ending. "The family woke to discover the beautiful tree. Although it wasn't much, the animals had shared all they had, and the family was grateful."

"That's why you waited to decorate the tree."

She nodded. "We wait until Yule, the longest night of the year."

"December 21st."

"Your turn to answer a question." Morgan looked at him point blank. "What did you do?"

"What does it matter?" He stared at his book, then wrote something in his notebook.

She shrugged. "I just wondered."

"They think I stole something."

"Did you?" she asked.

The corners of his mouth turn down as he shrugged his shoulders.

"Why?" Morgan prodded, hoping to catch him off guard.

He looked more quizzical than guilty. "I don't know," he said slowly.

Morgan's mom appeared from one of the clinic's back rooms. "I think you should take Lucan with you to give the animals their Yule presents before it gets too dark." Leaving the animals something special on the winter solstice was another annual tradition Morgan really enjoyed. And not one she was particularly interested in sharing with Lucan.

"Sure, Mom." Morgan and Lucan grabbed their coats, hats and gloves, and headed for the center's large barn.

"Have you got all your holiday shopping done?" Morgan asked Lucan by way of conversation as they loaded hay, seed, corn, grain, apples, and other treats into a cart.

Lucan shook his head. "I don't see the point."

She stared at him. "What do you mean? It's supposed to be time of good cheer and glad tidings; a time for giving."

"Christmas is for kids."

Morgan was stunned. *I'm a kid. Well, maybe not so much anymore,* she admitted. *But I like Yule. And, I want Christmas.*

In silence, they loaded bird houses handmade from cobs of corn and decorated with sunflower and pumpkin seeds. It looked like the mice had started early on some of the seasonal gifts. The last thing they put in the cart was a wreath made of colorful Indian corn, the husks of which fanned the outside of the ring like a brilliant sunburst.

They both reached for the long handle of the cart. Morgan snatched her hand back when his hand accidentally brushed hers. She abruptly turned, leading the way toward the pens.

Lucan followed Morgan, dragging the cart. They walked in silence as they headed for the center's long Nature Trail which housed animals that couldn't be released back into the wild. Most of these animals had suffered some sort of permanent injury. They became the center's Animal Educators, and were used in nearly every program to teach people to care for and about wildlife.

Snow crunched under the kids' feet as they walked from pen to pen filling each bowl and feeding platform. "This is Jerome." Morgan broke the silence, stopping in front of one of the better outfitted pens — that is, one that contained a bathtub, complete with ramp, and what looked like a two-story wooden doghouse."

Lucan searched the pen for the apparently invisible occupant. "Who's Jerome? I've never seen anybody in here. I thought this pen was empty."

Morgan walked into the pen with a bunch of grapes, stood in front of the house, and clucked her tongue. "That's because Jerome's nocturnal. He prefers to sleep hidden under the bathtub during the daytime." She clucked a little louder.

A tiny black nose poked its way out of the small doorway, wiggling about to test the air to see if there was anything worth bothering to get up for. Morgan plucked a grape, bit it in half, and brushed the animal's nose with the wet sweetness she knew was his favorite. He blinked in the waning daylight as he pushed his black and white head out of his warm home and accepted the treat.

Lucan took a step back, shocked to find himself so close to a skunk. "That's Jerome?" He glanced nervously back to the pen door trying to decide if he could make it out without getting sprayed.

"Don't worry." Morgan handed the skunk another grape. "He's more interested in his snack than he is in you. Besides, he's here because he was de-scented illegally."

"De-scented?" Lucan stammered. "You can do that?"

"Yes, by removing the glands under his tail." Morgan stroked the long, soft fur from head to tail, now that the animal had fully emerged from its home. "Of course, that makes him defenseless in the wild." She put a large bunch of grapes onto the pen floor, and filled the bowl with an extra helping of dog food.

"Don't be greedy," she told the skunk as she got up to go. "Leave some for Sasha."

"Who's Sasha?" Lucan searched the pen for a second skunk.

"His girlfriend."

"There are *two* of them in here?"

"Not exactly. Sasha is a wild skunk who lives under the pen." Morgan led the way out of the enclosure. "Well, under the skunk condo, to be precise. She showed up one winter, pregnant and looking for a hand-out. Jerome always has plenty of food, so I guess he didn't mind sharing with her and, later, with her babies. When her kids left, she decided she'd stay on. They've been together ever since."

"I thought all the pens had chain link under them so nothing could dig in and hurt the residents?"

"They do. Jerome and Sasha are together, but not." Morgan showed Lucan where the wild skunk had burrowed under the wire so she could sleep just below her captive mate. "They sleep in the same den, but separate. She wanders the neighborhood all night, and comes back to him every morning. It's kinda sweet."

"A good arrangement," said Lucan thoughtfully. "She keeps him company, and he keeps her well fed."

Morgan and Lucan finished in the late afternoon, hanging the beautiful corn wreath at the very end of the trail's long gravel path. Morgan looked around. It was getting pretty dark. She bowed her head to say her quick prayer. "I am grateful for all that I have. Let me ever be mindful of the needs of others. And do my part."

They started back to the barn to drop off the empty cart without speaking. It was beginning to snow, and a strange wind picked up. Morgan squinted. The world was disappearing in a flurry of white. The path was quickly covered and, for the first time in her life, Morgan was lost in a place she knew like the face that stared back at her from the mirror.

"How do we get back?" Lucan shouted over the rising wind.

"I don't know." Morgan shielded her eyes with her gloved hand trying to see something familiar. "I think it's this way."

"Follow me." A strange voice said.

Morgan stared at Lucan, confused. "What did you say?"

"I didn't say anything."

She searched for the owner of the voice, but all Morgan could see was swirling snowflakes.

"Follow me."

Morgan was certain she'd heard something.

"I think I heard it, too." The growing storm swallowed their voices. Lucan sounded far away, even though he was standing right next to her.

Suddenly, a four-point black-tailed stag materialized from the storm. Morgan caught her breath. Although they had raised a lot of fawns at the wildlife center, she'd never been so close to a fully antlered buck before. *Is this one we raised?* The animal was easily five-foot tall, hoof to antler, and looked like it weighed over a hundred pounds. A long, jagged white scar streaked across its left shoulder. *An old bullet wound?* Morgan didn't realize she'd taken a step forward to get a better look at the deer until Lucan's hand closed around her arm and pulled her back.

"Careful," he warned.

"Follow me or die." The stag turned, flicking its short black-and-white tail like a beacon.

"That's not possible." Lucan blinked.

So he'd heard it, too! Morgan knew animals talked. She had understood them, more or less, her whole life. It was the clear use of *words* that caught her off guard. Most interspecies communication was through thoughts and feelings. An innate ability in children, the gift was lost to most adults as their minds got busier and more crowded. Morgan intended to keep her gift. "To where?" she asked the stag.

The animal didn't answer as it moved ahead, forcing them to follow or be lost in the growing storm. As they walked, the snow continued to deepen. *We can't still be at the wildlife center,* Morgan thought. *But we can't be anywhere else.* She pulled her coat tightly around herself, glad for the hood that kept her ears warm. Lucan's face was also hidden by his oversize parka.

"Has this ever happened before?" she heard him ask.

"No."

"Are we heading back to the clinic?" His breath condensed in the cold air.

"I don't think so." Morgan still didn't recognize where they were, or where they were going. And she was getting colder and more tired. How much farther was the stag taking them?

She stumbled on a half-buried rock. Lucan caught her hand before she fell. Her fingers tingled unexpectedly, despite her glove. Focused on the stag, Lucan continued to hold her hand even after she'd steadied herself.

The deer stopped, allowing them catch up. The snow subsided. For some reason she didn't quite understand, Morgan was a little disappointed when Lucan let go. They stood with the stag between them looking down a shallow ravine. At the bottom, amidst a grove of trees made bare by winter, was a small log cabin. Smoke curled from its chimney. A yellow light glowed invitingly from its small windows. Four short stair steps led to a simple front porch surrounded by a railed deck. Two well-used wooden chairs flanked an equally worn table.

"They can't see you," the stag told them. "Or hear you."

"Who?" Lucan glanced around.

The animal motioned his head toward the cabin. Lucan started down the slope, as if compelled by some unseen force.

"Where are you going?" Morgan followed. She looked back to where the stag had been, but the animal was gone. "Why?" she asked Lucan when she'd caught up to him. "What's there?"

"I don't know."

When they reached the cabin and climbed its few stair steps, they could hear people inside. Without hesitation, Lucan walked *right through* the closed front door.

Morgan gasped. *How did he do that? How did he know he could?* She reached her hand out to touch what she, up to a few moments ago, had believed to be a solid barrier. Her hand disappeared through the door. She gasped and pulled it back, wiggling her fingers to make sure they were still all there. Satisfied, she followed Lucan inside.

"Holy smokes!" She was inside a small room that looked like it served as both a kitchen and an eating area. A stack of logs sat next to a wood burning stove that was being used to cook food and to keep the little house warm. A stocky woman, her brown hair rolled up in a bun on top of her head, poured water from a pitcher sitting next to the sink. Through an open door she saw two beds separated by a heavy blanket hung between them. In the kitchen a piece of oak with four partially burned candles adorned the center of the sturdy wooden table. Morgan recognized the Yule log.

A red-haired man was mesmerizing his children, both of whom appeared younger than Morgan and Lucan, with stories about the ghosts of Yule and the birth of the sun. The wind, howling outside, added atmosphere to the spooky tales.

The windows and doors were decorated with garlands of holly and ivy, cedar and pine. Morgan inhaled deeply. She could smell everything—the bread in the oven, the stew cooking in the pot, and the herbs hanging from the ceiling to dry. Her stomach rumbled. She looked at Lucan, who seemed to be watching the family captivated. "Do you know these people?" she whispered.

"No."

Morgan felt eyes on her. She glanced at the children. "Is she staring at us?" The little girl's eyes were wide and seemed locked on her and Lucan. *She is watching us.* Until that moment, she had been certain she and Lucan had gone unnoticed.

"Papa, I see them," the child said and pointed directly at Morgan and Lucan.

"Who, my little Anoushka?" His voice was deep and strong.

The five year old slid behind her father. "The ghosts."

Morgan and Lucan froze. "She *can* see us." Morgan whispered, in case the girl could hear them, too.

"Not possible," Lucan said. "The stag told us we were invisible." But Morgan saw doubt in his face.

"No worries, my little darling." The girl's mother took a bundle of sage from the windowsill and set the end to smoking. She walked around the room, waving the pungent incense until the smoke lightly filled the space. "With the power I have in me, negative energy I banish thee. Ghosts be gone, you are no more. Holly guards every door!"

Morgan caught her breath when the woman blew the smoke right into their faces. She looked down at herself and Lucan. "Nothing happened. We're still here."

But to the eyes of the little girl, it seemed they had disappeared. Comforted, she climbed into her father's lap at the table. Father led them in a Meal Blessing, after which Mother dished out large helpings of steaming hot stew and platefuls of warm bread and butter. The meal looked plain but hearty, and the family finished it in no time.

Bang. Bang. Bang.

Morgan and Lucan jumped, startled. They both looked at each other wondering who could be at this remote front door at this late hour.

"Ho, ho, ho."

The children squealed and raced to see who could get to the door first. They threw it open for heavy-set man with a full white beard and mustache. He was wearing a woolen coat, dyed the color of rust and lined with fur. He carried a small bundle. "It's Nicolai!" they cried.

Morgan couldn't believe her own eyes. "Is that who I think it is?"

"That's not possible." Lucan's response was sharp. "He doesn't exist. It's got to be a neighbor, or maybe a relative."

Morgan saw no familiarity in any of their faces. *It might be, but I don't think so.*

Lucan became hard as they watched the happy family. The old man passed out nuts, dried fruits, and sweets, a carved comb for Mother, tobacco for Father, a wooden horse for the little girl and a toy knife for the boy.

"Let's get out of here." Lucan's voice was cold as he pushed Morgan toward the door. Before she could object, they were outside and once again standing on the porch. A horse-drawn sleigh sat in front of the cabin. The shaggy pony turned to look at them, unfazed by the fact that they'd just passed through the front door.

"Hey, it can see us." Morgan pushed aside her annoyance with Lucan. Apparently both animals *and* children could see them. *How cool!*

The snow had stopped, and the sky was clear and bright. "What's with you?" Morgan complained as Lucan continued to push her past the horse and back up the hillside. The pony watched them go. She protested. "I was having a good time. I wanted to stay."

"We need to get back." Lucan stomped past her in the direction they had come.

"Why?" Morgan fumed as she struggled to keep up with Lucan's long and hurried steps. It was clear he didn't *care* what she wanted, or that she was enjoying herself.

They were both panting by the time they reached the top of the hill. *Which way now?* Morgan looked for the stag, but the animal was nowhere to be found. They turned a full circle, but the tracks they'd made to the cabin had been covered by new snow.

"That way." Lucan pointed towards the woods.

"How do you know?"

He set his jaw. "I just do."

Morgan and Lucan walked for a good long time without speaking, putting distance between them and the cheerful family. Her anger cooled the longer they walked. Morgan started to feel sorry for the bitter boy. She shivered, but not from the cold.

Lucan wore an expression Morgan had seen in too many adults, particularly at this time of year — one of anger and frustration. *I don't get it.* She pondered. *Why do so many people gripe about the winter holidays when they're all about hope and cheer?*

She followed the brooding boy through the dense forest. *Does he really know the way back,* she asked herself several times during their determined trek, *or are we just getting more lost?*

Lucan's shadow stretched between them, long and black, a sharp contrast to the white snow. Morgan stomped on Lucan's head with every step. It helped her keep up with his longer stride, and satisfied her growing impatience at the same time.

The moon must be full, she thought, looking up into the sky. But they weren't following a full moon; instead, she saw the brightest star she'd ever seen. *Is that what he's following?* She wondered. But she didn't see his eyes leave the horizon.

When they finally cleared the woods, a gravel path lay before them. Recognizing where they were, Morgan jogged past Lucan. She turned and smiled. "We're back at the wildlife center." Behind him, the forest they'd just traveled through was gone. She did a full circle, seeing only the familiar property, and their empty cart.

"Did that really happen?" Lucan stared up at the darkening sky. "We were there for hours, but it's just *starting* to get dark."

Morgan gazed up. He was right. The bright star was gone and the daylight was only just now receding into night, as if no time had passed while they had wandered.

Then she noticed the path, which was still mostly covered with snow. A chill crept up her spine. Their footprints had been nearly obliterated by a set of deeper ones. *Had someone been following us?* The dark tracks circled as if they had lost their prey, then abandoned their search and left the grounds. Morgan's eyes followed the tracks to the edge of the property and caught sight of the stag near a grove of trees. She recognized it by the white streak on its shoulder, like a comet. It flicked its tail, turned, and disappeared.

"Morgan? Lucan? Where are you?" They heard her mother calling from the parking lot. "Aren't you done yet? It's time to go."

Lucan grabbed the cart handle, and they raced towards the clinic.

* * * * *

"You were on your first vision quest." Aunt Jackie smiled at her niece after the girl had finished telling them about her adventure. "Congratulations. Some people *never* manage to accomplish a true quest."

"But why today?" Morgan wondered if Yule had had anything to do with it. The dark season is one for dreaming and planning. "I've been meditating for months, trying to meet a totem animal."

"Maybe it wasn't your totem animal." Aunt Jackie offered. "Maybe it was Lucan's."

Morgan scowled. *You mean the first totem animal I meet isn't even there for me?* "What would the totem deer want with Lucan? He doesn't care about Yule, and he doesn't *believe* in Christmas. It's so unfair." She crossed her arms. "And why drag me along?"

"The deer didn't drag you along, dear." Her mother explained. "It sounds to me like you *facilitated* the vision." After a minute, she handed her daughter a wrapped gift. "From Aunt Jackie and me."

Morgan brightened. One of the best things about celebrating Yule *and* Christmas was the presents. She got one on Yule, opened presents with family on Christmas eve, and got a stocking from Santa Claus on Christmas morning. She pulled off the white bow and tore open the blue and silver wrapping paper. The box inside revealed a necklace from which hung a sterling charm--a stag. Morgan's jaw dropped. "How did you know?" She looked up at her mom and Aunt Jackie, who wore the same soft smile.

"We didn't," her mom assured her.

"Just happenstance." Aunt Jackie shrugged with a twinkle in her eye.

* * * * *

At midnight on Christmas Eve, Morgan looked down from the choir balcony at the capacity crowd that filled the small Lutheran church. *Typical*, she thought. *People who don't show up all year turn up at Christmas and Easter.*

Morgan scolded herself for her snarky thoughts. Mom always says, "What you send out into the world comes back to you." It wasn't like Morgan managed to get to church every week either.

The church hummed with holiday energy, and Morgan was enjoying it. She wiggled her fingers at her mom and aunt, who sat in pews in the middle of the building. They wanted the best view of her, and the best acoustics.

Christmas ornaments could be seen in every corner. The decorating committee had outdone itself again this year. White string lights glittered around each of the stained glass windows. Red bows tacked to the edge of the pews lined the center aisle that led to the altar. To the left, the pulpit was wrapped with scented pine and cedar garland. On the right stood the Christmas tree the kids had decorated at the Bazaar. It was adorned with doves and angels, along with the usual holiday ornaments. Under the tree was the carved Nativity scene purchased directly from woodcarvers in Germany—very appropriate for a Lutheran church.

Morgan blinked, taking another look at the large cut fir. *Where is the Christmas star?* She tried to remember if she'd seen it at the Bazaar, recalled the flash of the reporter's camera, and the sharp glint that had momentarily affected her vision. It had practically called out to her. She was sure the star had been there. *And so had Lucan!* Morgan looked to her left, searching the black clad choir singers for Lawren. *Is that what was stolen?* She mouthed the words to her best friend, who soberly nodded her head, *yes*.

Why would anyone steal the crystal star tree topper? Morgan wondered. Granted, it was one of the nicest of the ornaments in the church's vast collection, but it couldn't be all that valuable. Most of the decorations were donated, after all.

Morgan searched the crowd for Lucan. He and his family sat almost directly under the balcony near the doors. She had to lean way over to spot them. He was dressed in a blue sweater that accented his dark hair and . . . *blue eyes*. He was looking right at her. She caught her breath and snapped up straight, flushing.

She tried to imagine Lucan stealing the fancy topper, but couldn't see it. *Why would he?* The star was a multi-point glass ornament, whose only distinguishing feature was an unusual red heart that seemed to float inside. It didn't even light up, like many of the modern fiber optic ones. She willed herself to come up with some reasonable explanation, but all she could do was remind herself that Lucan hadn't exactly admitted to committing the crime. His words echoed in her mind. "They think I stole something." She frowned. *Maybe I just don't want to believe Lucan would rob a church.* She shivered, remembering the stag and the footprints in the snow on Yule. *I didn't imagine those tracks following us either. Who knows what would have happened if that totem animal hadn't shown up when it did?*

The choir conductor tapped his music stand, calling them to attention. The organ started playing. The start of the Christmas service cut off her jumbled thoughts.

Sparks that Inspire

January was spent keeping the animals' water bowls and food from freezing and replacing old Christmas trees with new ones donated by local growers after the holidays. Lucan now worked at the wildlife center one day a week. He spent most of the month with Morgan's Uncle Rick, removing wooden bases from last year's trees and attaching them to fresh cut ones. By the end of the month new pine and fir trees filled each animal's pen with glorious scent and new places to climb and hide.

Lucan was dropped off and picked up by one parent or the other without either one of them actually getting out of the car. Morgan thought it was strange that she never met them. By February she knew no more about the sullen boy than she had when he'd first been brought to the wildlife center. Guilty or not, Lucan was doing his time without issue.

* * * * *

"These guys reek." Lucan scrunched his nose as he scooped soiled shavings from one of the tiered aquariums that housed the wildlife center's feeder mice. He replaced them with fresh smelling pine. He was not enjoying his first foray into cleaning mice.

"Yeah, the lady who cleans them goes on vacation a lot." Morgan was across the small room cleaning the stainless steel animal cages. A hawk watched her warily from the pen next door. "Why do you red-tails have to shoot poop?" she complained as she scrubbed gooey white feces from the bars and the splattered linoleum floor.

"How many mice do you have?"

"These in here," Morgan nodded toward the twelve aquariums that lined one wall of the room. Each clear Plexiglas tank held six to twenty mice. "And about a dozen more pens in the mouse shed outside. Keeping two separate colonies makes sure we don't lose all our mice, should something happen to one of them."

He took a deep breath and exhaled slowly. "That's a lot of stinky mice to clean."

"Hurry." Sonny appeared seemingly from thin air.

Morgan jumped. The elderly volunteer had a habit of surprising people.

"I'm almost finished with the animal care." Sonny was just a little too chipper so early in the morning. "Today is burn day!" The volunteer twirled dramatically in her usual overalls and colorful tie-dyed shirt, leaving the room with a swish of her hip-length gray braid.

"Burn day?" Lucan asked Morgan.

"Yup. We burn last year's Christmas trees." Morgan dropped the rag she was using into her cleaning bucket.

"We've got to keep an eye on Sonny," Morgan grinned. "I'm not sure she isn't a closet pyromaniac."

Lucan chuckled.

Morgan enjoyed his soft laugh. It was something she didn't hear too often from the serious boy. *I have to admit, he's kinda cute when he smiles.* Despite the fact that she didn't know much about him, Morgan found herself reluctantly attracted to his blue eyes and wavy black hair. She closed the pen she'd cleaned and lined with fresh newspaper. "Since we have to get rid of the old trees any way, Mom and Aunt Jackie make a kind of ritual out of it. It's really pretty fun."

After finishing their chores Lucan and Morgan grabbed their parkas and headed outside. In front of the barn was a large round spot of black soot where they did their burning. Last year's trees stood nearby like rusty and balding mummies, waiting to be disposed of.

Aunt Jackie dragged several of the trees onto the simple fire pit while Morgan's mom and Sonny watched. The volunteer's eyes sparkled. Morgan knew the elderly woman lived in an apartment in the city where no burning is allowed. The freezing mist that had everyone burrowed into their heavy coats made the day perfect for containing a small bonfire.

"This is the time of inspiration." Morgan's aunt's voice took a formal tone.

"Groundhog day?" Lucan was confused.

Morgan barely suppressed a giggle. "I guess a groundhog looking for his shadow is all they could come up with to incorporate the hope for an early spring."

"According to folklore," Morgan's mom explained, "if it's cloudy when a groundhog pokes its head from its den on this day, spring will come early; if it's sunny and the animal sees its shadow, it will retreat back into its burrow and winter will hang on for another six weeks."

"Candle-Mass. Festival of Flames. Imbolc. Winter's Ease." Sonny shrugged. "Whatever you want to call it, it's when the sun starts to make progress against the dark."

Morgan squirmed self-consciously. No one else she knew observed the turning of the seasons like they did. She covertly watched Lucan's face. *Just how crazy does he think we are?*

The boy looked confused. "So if it's a nice day winter hangs on? That doesn't really make any sense."

"It does sound kinda backward," Morgan admitted, "but it's actually warmer when the weather is overcast and the rains begin."

Aunt Jackie took a deep breath, letting it out solemnly. It condensed into a white plume before disappearing. Morgan could feel strength rising from the ground and encircling them. It thrilled and calmed her at the same time.

"It's still so cold and dark at this time of year," Jackie told them, "we like to remind ourselves to take heart." She looked around the circle, pausing briefly on each person's face. "Consider what you need to be inspired."

Morgan's mother smiled at Lucan and added. "Seems appropriate for an environmental center, don't you agree?"

"Besides," Sonny grinned and pulled out her box of long-stick matches. "It's fun to burn."

Morgan looked down at her feet to make sure the water hose was there. She was glad the rest of the old, dead trees stood a safe distance away, waiting to be incinerated one at a time.

Sonny lit the pile, then stepped back, clasping her hands together tightly in front of her lips. "Burn away the old and welcome the new," she said.

"Of what would you be rid?" Jackie asked. The dried wood caught quickly in a cacophony of popping and crackling. Flames shot toward the sky and gray smoke billowed. Sonny's gleaming eyes never left the scorching dance. She did look totally nuts.

As each tree turned to ash, Jackie added another. One by one the tree husks kept the fire burning intensely, until they were all reduced to cinder. Morgan stole a quick glance at Lucan. She wondered what was holding his joy hostage. *What would he get rid of, if he could?*

Morgan squirted floating embers with water when they were done, deep in thought. For a while the world seemed to slow, suspending rain, breath, and ash. And then she realized what she herself needed. *I need to rid myself of my own doubt. I need to find out who stole that ornament. And, I need to know why.* She was pulled out of her trance by the acrid smell of smoke and a new determination.

Her mother pulled a couple of thin packages of plain paper from under her coat and handed one to her daughter and one to Lucan. A sparkler was tied to each parcel with jute. Aunt Jackie handed a sparkler to her sister and Sonny. Lucan looked at Morgan uncertain, as he reached for the unexpected gift.

"As the sunlight grows and lights the coming days," Jackie lit her sparkler and passed the matches around the circle for everyone to do the same while she finished, "find the light that shines within."

When the firework had burned down, Morgan nodded to Lucan and they tore open their packages, throwing the paper wrapping into the hot coals. Inside each was a blank notebook. Morgan smiled. It was the same gift every year. "To record your ideas and plans," she explained, "or whatever you want."

"Hoot. Hoot. Hoot." Mom's distinctive cell phone ring called her back to work.

"Fun's over." The indomitable Sonny was as happy after the bonfire as she'd been anticipating it. A bundle of positive energy, the volunteer tended the embers as the others headed back to the clinic.

"State Police found a bobcat caught in a trap and need help getting it out," Mom said as she stuffed her cell phone back to the rear pocket of her jeans.

"You mean they want drugs." Jackie had a way of getting right to the point.

Morgan was so excited it barely registered when Lucan took her parka and hung back onto the coat rack just inside the door. *A bobcat!*

"It's a little late in the day to anesthetize anything." Mom shook her head looking outside at the darkening sky, "unless you want to be out all night waiting for it to wake."

"If you want, I'll call your mother to pick you up later," Jackie told Lucan.

The boy nodded. His face told them he wouldn't miss this for the world.

"I guess I'll man the fort." Aunt Jackie turned on her computer and shot her twin sister a semi-cautionary look. "Try not to let anyone get bit."

The long drive to the bobcat led from the highway to a two-way street, to a one-way road, to a dirt path, stopping only once to meet and follow the State Police Game Officer's car into the deep woods. It was already getting dark.

Morgan and Lucan sat in the back seats. He stared out his window without speaking. *I can't figure him out,* she thought. *Just when I think he's thawed a little, he clams back up and disappears again, like he's afraid of saying something.* Impatient, she shook her head and turned to her mom. "How did they even find this bobcat?"

"The usual way." Her mother glanced at her through the rear-view mirror, "walking the dog."

By the time the caravan finally stopped, Morgan was relieved to escape the confines of the car. Her backside was getting numb.

With his close cropped hair, clean shaven face, and perfectly pressed uniform, Officer Kincade looked like one of those Ken dolls—the plastic counterpart to the pseudo-perfect Barbie Morgan couldn't stand. "It's a short hike from here," he said in a smooth voice.

Morgan's mother pulled their standard trapping equipment out of the back of their SUV. She gave a long-handled net and a pair of heavy gloves to Lucan, and a heavy blanket to Morgan.

Morgan scowled without looking at her mother. *What? Lucan gets to hold the net?* Morgan disliked sharing the cool jobs, though she knew her mother usually had her reasons. She glanced at the darkening sky. A thin fog was starting to roll in.

Kincade led the way with a strong flashlight. Morgan shivered. She had the creepy feeling they were being watched. Scanning the area, she didn't see or hear anything except the crunching of their feet in old leaves and twigs. No one else seemed to notice.

The handsome officer signaled them to stop at a small clearing. In the center crouched the trapped bobcat. The animal glared at them, turned and jumped as they approached; it was pulled up short by the snap-trap that firmly held its front paw. The cat faced them again and hissed, threatening.

"I wasn't sure what to do. I didn't want to get bitten, or cause the animal more injury." Concern cracked the young officer's perfect facade. "I hope I didn't wait too long."

"I'm glad you called for help rather than try this yourself," Mom assured him. "It may be small for a wild cat, but it's pretty aggressive."

The veterinarian took a cautious step toward the cat to study the situation. Now it was all about the animal. "At least the trap doesn't have teeth," she said, "or the animal might suffer irreparable injury in its struggle to get away."

Morgan strained to see in the dimming light. The smooth jaws of the trap looked like it had barely snagged the animal; although it was clamped onto several of the bobcat's toes, just enough to hold it captive. Metal clattered against the chain that held the snare fast to the ground as the bobcat tried to pull away again. Morgan drew in a low hissing breath, mentally begging the cat not to hurt itself. She exhaled slowly, sending calming thoughts to the trapped feline.

"Do you have a dart gun?" Kincade asked.

"No." Mom shook her head. "Dart guns are usually reserved for much larger animals." Tending mostly to smaller creatures — raccoon, squirrel, rabbit, raptors, and the occasional bobcat, the wildlife center didn't even own the expensive, seldom used piece of equipment. "Besides, we don't want to be here all night waiting for the cat to wake up."

Mom did a quick scan of the area before concentrating on the feline once more. "And I don't want to take it out of its territory or away from its mate, if it has one."

The game officer's thick eyebrows furrowed. He didn't look certain about any of this.

Goosebumps walked up Morgan's spine as she stared into the dense shrubbery. *Is that what's watching us? A mate?* She thought she saw a flash of tiny, green-gold lights, and squinted towards the lower branches of a nearby tree. *I'm not imaging things. Those are eyes, and they're staring right at us.*

We're here to help. Morgan sent the mental message to the hidden animal, but she doubted it was in a receiving mood. Nevertheless, the forest seemed to quiet, as if holding its breath to watch. Morgan forced herself to turn her attention back to the trapped cat. If they were being spied on by the bobcat's mate, the animal was too small to even consider attacking them. *Right?* She suppressed the niggling doubt creeping around the edge of her mind.

Her mother harbored no such concerns. She donned her protective gear and took the net from Lucan. "Put the gloves on," she ordered.

He slipped the oversized welder's gloves over his hands, and looked back uncertainly.

"Once I've netted it, take the handle and push it flat to the ground so the cat can't move." She demonstrated. When she was sure Lucan knew what he had to do, Mom turned to Officer Kincade. "When we've immobilized the cat, you'll have to free it from the trap. You're most familiar with the device."

Mom walked slowly toward the captured animal. "I'm counting on you," she told Lucan, "to keep the cat from doing any more damage to the foot. Get only as close as you have to."

Lucan nodded, swallowing hard.

Mom dropped the net over the animal and, in one quick motion, twisted the mesh tight. The bobcat growled and hissed loudly. As far as the cat was concerned, it was fighting for its life. "Now," Mom ordered.

Lucan took over the net, grabbing the handle at the far end and pushing it flat against the ground, preventing the cat from struggling.

Morgan hastily handed the blanket to her mother, who tossed the heavy cover over the netted animal. With the blanket between them, Mom sandwiched the cat between her hands and knees, pressing the animal to the ground. The bobcat was immobile. Only its fore leg with the trapped paw was exposed.

"You should be able to safely remove the snare now." Her mom told the awestruck officer, stirring him to action. He fumbled for the release lever, pulled the jaws of the trap apart, and freed the bobcat.

The cat yanked its arm under the cover, growling and hissing in its struggle to get free.

"Is the foot broken?" Lucan's voice was thin.

"There's no bleeding or exposed bone," Mom explained, "which is good because I can't splint it. The toes will have to heal on their own."

"Everyone back away." Mom pulled off the blanket when they were at a safe distance, and freed the animal from the net. The bobcat hunched its back, facing its captors with pinned ears. It snarled and spit at them, ready to fight. When no one moved, it dared to look for an escape, then launched away, vanishing into the nearby shrubbery. If any toes *were* broken, they didn't seem to slow the animal down.

A loud clatter from the branches startled them. They heard it chase after the freed bobcat. Both animals disappeared in the growing fog like ghosts.

Kincade ran his hand through his ruffled hair, shaking his head and smiling. "That was a lot easier than I thought it would be."

"Easier is usually the best way." Mom collected their gear and handed it to Lucan.

"That was awesome." Lucan forgot himself and beamed at Morgan, blue eyes sparkling. "I've never seen anything like it." His damp hair curled wildly around his face.

Morgan grinned back, folding the blanket. *He's really cute when he drops the attitude.*

Lucan wasn't nearly as reticent on the drive back to the wildlife center, recounting every moment of the experience he apparently considered "once-in-a-lifetime."

I guess it is kinda cool. Having grown up around the animals, Morgan sometimes forgot how extraordinary her life could be. It was fun seeing it through Lucan's eyes, and made her feel very special indeed.

* * * * *

"You should've seen it." Lawren pulled out a chair and plopped down next to Morgan at the library during study break. "The church office was totally trashed. It's going to take Mary a week to put it all back together,"

Morgan was shocked. *Who would vandalize a church? Why?* She felt a twinge of guilt when her first thought was, *Lucan.* "Was anything broken or stolen?" she asked her best friend.

"That's the funny thing." Lawren pushed her glasses up the bridge of her nose. "As far as Mom can tell, nothing is missing or destroyed." She went on to describe the damage in as much colorful detail as she could. Lawren had a flair for the dramatic. That's what you get when your mother's a minister and your father's a big-time defense attorney.

"What about the church?" Morgan asked.

Lawren shook her head. "They didn't touch the church."

"Why break into the office and not the church?" Morgan wondered. "What were they looking for?"

"I dunno." Lawren shrugged. "There's nothing but a bunch of office stuff, and junk in an old storeroom—seasonal decorations for service, mostly."

Morgan pursed her lips. With no idea *what* the culprit was looking for, they couldn't even guess *who* might be looking. No time to start naming suspects.

"I've got to help clean up after school today." Lawren opened her textbook. "Can you come over and help?"

"Sure." Morgan doodled in her notebook, unable to concentrate on her studies. *Even If Lucan wasn't the thief, what, if anything, did he have to do with the break-in?* She was convinced he was still involved somehow.

"I'm going to the dance with Thano." Lawren whispered, abruptly changing the subject. She glanced over her shoulder to make sure no one had heard her. The school librarian gave them the evil eye.

Morgan smiled innocently at the woman behind the checkout counter. "You're going with Nathan Stone?" She turned to her friend and charged, incredulous. "I thought *you and I* were going." The two girls had been going to after-school activities together for as long as she could remember.

Lawren stared at her book red-faced. Neither knew what to say as awkward silence stretched between them.

"It's okay." Morgan sighed and let her friend off the hook. "I'll figure something out." She looked around the room to see who was there and caught Paige's attention. *Great! Just what I need.* She shrank down in her seat hoping to bury herself behind her books. The popular Paige wore make-up and the latest fashion, neither of which Morgan gave much of a hoot about.

Paige pulled out the chair next to Morgan, not caring who heard the loud scrape of wooden feet on vinyl floor. She and her gang of cronies surrounded Morgan and Lawren, filling every seat at the small table.

"Hi, Paige." Morgan forced a smile. "What's up?"

"I was just wondering who you're going to the Valentine's Day dance with?" Paige flipped back her long brown hair. "I'm going with Zane."

Of course. The most popular boy in school. Way out of Morgan's league, Zane was good at practically everything. Basketball. Softball. Track. *And,* he was cute. What he saw in Paige, Morgan couldn't fathom.

"I'm going with Thano." Lawren's soft voice tried to rescue Morgan, who didn't have a date.

"Who's Thano?" Red-headed Megan fell for the decoy.

"Bor-ing." Paige pretend-yawned, tapping her hand over her open mouth.

Most of the kids in the small town went to one church or another, but Lawren was different. Being the preacher's daughter, she practiced her religion more than most. In some ways Morgan envied her friend's faith. Though Morgan enjoyed her family's flexible spirituality, she found herself questioning everything.

"So, who did you say you were going with?" Paige pressed, obviously more interested in Morgan's prospects, or lack thereof, than curious about Lawren's new guy.

"She's going with me."

Morgan jumped. *How did he sneak up on me?*

"That is, if she'll ever say yes." Lucan leaned over between them, resting one hand on the corner of each of their chairs.

"Uh, sure." At the moment, Morgan didn't see any other options. Being one year older than all of them, Lucan was a bit of a mystery. And being cute didn't hurt.

"Can I talk to you for a minute?" Lucan snagged her book bag off the back of her chair before she could answer.

Morgan stood up, hugging her notepad and textbook to her chest. She was glad for the rescue, even by him.

"I gotta go too." Lawren grabbed her own pack and beat a hasty retreat.

Morgan found herself being led to an empty table where they wouldn't be overheard. Lucan dropped her bag onto the table and sat down.

She sat down and waited for Lucan to tell her what was going on. She searched his clear blue eyes for answers to questions that dogged her. As usual, there were none.

She thought rescuing the bobcat together had broken the ice between them, but they hadn't talked much since then. Even at the wildlife center. In fact, it looked like he'd gone right back to avoiding her. She squirmed. "You didn't tell anyone, did you?" she asked.

Somehow, he knew exactly what she meant. "What? That you're a witch that can teleport to another time and place? That you stand around bonfires casting spells? Or that you rescue animals in the middle of the night like some superhero?"

She jumped to her own defense. "I'm not a witch. We didn't cast any spells. And . . . um . . . well, not every night."

"Besides," he scoffed as if he couldn't believe she'd even asked the question. "Who would I tell?" Awkwardness stretched between them. He brought the conversation back. "You know we kinda *have* to go to the dance together now," he said, "even though I hate Valentine's Day."

"What's with you?" she snapped. Just when she thought she was starting to like him, she found herself annoyed again. "You don't believe in Christmas. You hate Valentine's Day." *Do you hate everything I love?*

Lucan picked at his fingernails. "Not because of you," he said quietly. "In fact, going with you will make the dance kinda all right."

Morgan felt her face flush. Any thought of demanding to know *why* he hated the holidays was suddenly lost. *Did he just say he* wanted *to go with me?*

Lucan picked up his oversized blue book bag, got up, and left without looking at her. "I'll see you there."

* * * * *

"Don't worry about washing your hands." A pretty blonde high school girl smiled as she stamped Morgan's hand heavily with a big red heart, then counted and put her money in metal change box. Morgan rubbed the spot on her hand, but the ink was already set. "It'll be a week before you manage to wash it off," said the girl, ready to ink the next person in line.

She's having just a little too much fun. Morgan was pushed by a group of chattering pre-teens through the door and into the decorated auditorium. She looked around the crowded room. *Wow. There are a lot more kids here than I thought.* The usual Valentine's Day décor — paper hearts, balloons, and streamers in red, white, and gold — filled the room. Loud music blared from speakers designed to do little more than announce the score at sporting events.

Circling the perimeter of the room to avoid the dance floor, Morgan headed for the refreshment table. She wasn't hungry, but it would give her something to do. *Chocolate chip cookies make everything better.*

She waved at Lawren, who was dancing with a geeky-looking guy with glasses. At least, it sorta looked like dancing. She didn't remember Thano looking quite so dorky in church. *Music doesn't bring out the best in everyone*, she thought, taking a sip of her punch and scanning the room. *At least Thano is dancing.* She noticed that most of the dancers were girls. The boys loitered around the edges, horsing around with each other.

A tap on her shoulder made her jump. She spilled her drink, narrowly missing her dress. She turned to see who had snuck up on her. Lucan was much closer than she was comfortable with. The room was suddenly too warm. Lucan looked handsome in his navy jacket and a new pair of black jeans. He shouted over the music. "Do you want to dance?"

She nodded. With two left feet, she wasn't exactly a good dancer. She usually preferred to dance in the center with the girls, letting the music wash away any awkwardness.

They had only been dancing thirty seconds when the song changed to a ballad. Morgan faltered when Lucan put his hands on her waist, after putting hers on his shoulders. They stood as far apart as possible.

"Morgan's an unusual name for a girl." Lucan broached the uncomfortable chasm between them.

"It means 'of the sea'." Morgan offered a weak smile and shrugged her shoulders. "Ironic, since I get awful motion sickness."

"I guess your mom couldn't have known."

He didn't ask what it means. She could've kicked herself before coming up with a quick, if not brilliant, answer. "Comes in handy when I don't want people I haven't met to know whether I'm a girl or a guy." She bit her lip. *And when would that be?* Unable to think of anything else, she returned the question. "Lucan's kind of a different name."

"It's actually Lucas." He looked into her face. For a moment, he seemed lost in a happy memory. "When I was really little my parents used to tell me 'Luke can' a lot. Luke can do this, and Luke can do that. I mixed it up, and started calling myself Lucan. I guess it stuck."

"You don't talk about your parents much."

Lucan stiffened. Apparently that was the wrong subject.

"Not much to tell," he said. "They fight a lot now."

"Is that why you hate Valentine's Day?" Morgan knew a lot of kids whose parents fought, and it often made them bitter over the holidays.

Lucan gave a quick nod.

"I'm glad it's just me and Mom." Morgan held her breath and waited for him to ask about her father. To her relief, he didn't. With so many "divided families," at least that's what her teacher's called them; she found few people ever asked. There was no father to track. Her mother had explained years ago how she had not found Mr. Right, despite the fact she had wanted a child. Morgan was a "gift from God via A.I. (Artfully Inspired by science)." She wasn't ashamed of her unconventional beginning, but she didn't offer to explain it.

The music stopped. Her ears rang. She looked into his face, and he didn't turn away. It seemed the right time to ask. "Why did you steal the tree topper?"

He took a breath, looking like he might finally tell her the truth. Before he could answer however, the school's heavyset principal climbed to the stage, barely managing the stairs in her over-tight dress. She did a princess wave as she walked to the microphone, cleared her throat, and addressed the kids in a nasally voice. "Welcome to the Valentine's Day dance. Help yourself to punch and cookies. Please stay in the gym, and be respectful or you will be asked to leave." She turned before remembering. "Oh, don't forget to hand out your Valentine cards."

The crowd rumbled as kids reached into their purses, bags, and pockets, pulling out cards and small gifts addressed to friends. The music started again.

Morgan and Lucan looked at each other and blushed. She pulled out the two cards she had made—one for him, and one for her best friend, Lawren. She handed him his. He pulled a single card from his coat pocket and handed it to her. Neither broke the envelope seals. *What if it's something really personal? What if he doesn't like it?* Lucan slid her unopened card into his pocket. Relieved, Morgan put hers in her purse, also unopened. She looked up at him and stammered awkwardly. "I have to give Lawren her card."

His smile seemed strained as he tilted his head in her friend's direction. "I think she's over by the punch."

Morgan wove her way toward the refreshment tables, nearly colliding with another couple. Flustered, she sidestepped and apologized, zigzagging her way to the tables and safety. She managed to avoid any more near-collisions. When she looked back, Lucan was gone. Disappointed, she took a deep breath and exhaled slowly. *I knew it. Probably couldn't wait to get out of here.* She couldn't help but wonder if she had driven him away with her question. She may as well have accused him outright. She hadn't asked *if* he'd stolen the tree topper, but *why*.

Looking around to make sure no one was watching, she pulled his card from her purse and opened it. Glued to the front of a white card was a glossy red heart in the center of which was an orange and yellow flame. *Happy Valentine's Day* was scrolled across the top. Inside he had written only three words. *You inspire me.* – Lucan

Spring Break-In

Morgan stared disappointed at the near-empty sign-up sheet she'd posted on the school bulletin board weeks ago. *Spring Clean-up on the Molalla River Corridor*. The annual trash collecting was sponsored by the Bureau of Land Management and featured the release of an animal by the wildlife center — a great horned owl this year.

"Looks like it's just you and me again." The perpetually upbeat Lawren didn't mind whether five or fifty people ever showed up.

That's so like Lawren, thought Morgan. Her friend's cheery style only added to her pixie-like qualities. That, and her tiny stature.

They heard a boy behind them jeering. "Thanks for cleaning up after us." Zane and a few of his football buddies loitered under a nearby tree. Paige clung to his arm laughing with them. "We camp up the Corridor all the time."

Although Morgan suspected the jock was baiting her, she didn't doubt he and his friends left litter for someone else to pick up. Her body tightened with anger and frustration. *I'm not picking up after those pigs*.

She stuffed her hands in her pockets, trying to regain her composure. *Yes, I am*. Morgan had to remind herself, *I'm doing this for the earth*. The worst part was feeling like she cleaned up after the same people year after year—the same campers and hikers leaving the same type of garbage in the same places. *Why can't they clean up after themselves? They carry the stuff in. What's so hard about carrying it out?*

"I like it in the Molalla River Corridor." Lawren ignored the taunting. "I like it even better when it's clean."

Morgan hooked her arm around her friend's and exhaled, letting her annoyance go with her breath. The insults faded away. *I'm doing it for us, too.*

On the day of the clean-up, the kids met at the school parking lot. Morgan was surprised to see Lucan . . . and he'd dragged Zane with him. She gawked at them. How had he managed that? The two of them were chatting like best buds. *Maybe I don't give Lucan enough credit*, she thought.

Lawren had also managed to convince Thano to help. With Morgan, that made five kids from the middle school that climbed into the van headed for the Molalla River Corridor. Before it pulled out of the parking lot, the driver opened the door for a panting Anna Wildling, who'd almost missed the bus. The girl pushed stray wisps of strawberry blonde hair that had escaped her long braid out of her face. She plopped down next to Morgan, smiling at her brightly.

Morgan smiled weakly at the younger girl before staring out the window to watch as the bus rolled past trees and bushes. The forest was waking up. Leaves were starting to unfurl. Buds were beginning to open. The world sparkled as sunlight glinted off wet roads, plants, other cars, everything. It would be a gorgeous day for a walk in the woods—if you overlook the picking up garbage part, of course.

"We're lucky." Lawren's face was reflected in the glass next to her, although her friend actually sat in the seat *behind* Morgan, next to Thano. "Last year it rained."

"It rains every year," Morgan grumbled. As a native Oregonian, the months of rain each year didn't bother her a bit.

Morgan glanced toward the back of the bus. Lucan and Zane were having a lively conversation about who knows what. She slouched down in her seat. *This is going to be a long day.*

"It's still wet, but at least it's sunny and warm." Anna didn't seem to notice Morgan's bad mood.

The bus slowed and turned into the parking lot. From there it would be a short hike to Aquila Vista.

"Welcome, everyone." A dark-skinned man sporting a black Mohawk haircut that ended in a ponytail greeted them as they got off the bus. "My name is Tommy Lightfoot. I'm with the Bureau of Land Management."

Morgan waved at him. He nodded with his usual smile — one that emanated from his soul and reflected in his eyes. She had known the Native American most of her life. Tommy was also a volunteer educator for the wildlife center and frequently helped them find the best release sites for recovered patients.

Tommy led them up a narrow walking path to a large log structure with tables and benches that offered protection from the rain and a place to sit. About thirty people waited for them. Other sign-up sheets had apparently had better results than Morgan's.

Not much taller than most of the kids, Tommy stood on one of the tables in order to be seen. "Welcome to Aquila Vista Education Center. You'll start and end your service day here, and be shuttled to various spots along the Corridor that need cleaning." He grabbed a yellow plastic garbage bag from the table next to him. "As you fill your bags, drop them along the roadside for our truck to collect. We have gloves, if you need them." Tommy pulled a pair of rubber gloves out of his back pocket and waved them overhead. "Be careful of any sharp objects. We don't want anyone to get an infection from a cut."

A five-year-old raised his hand, bouncing up and down. "What if we have to go to the bathroom?" His brother snickered and poked him in the ribs. Their mother intervened before it developed into something more.

"We have several outhouses along the trail," Tommy chuckled. "They're pretty nice, so don't be afraid to use them."

"We want to thank you all for being here today to help keep our forests clean." Tommy continued. "When we're finished this morning, we'll have a picnic lunch. The folks at the wildlife center will tell us a little about the owls that live along the Corridor. After we eat, they're going to release an owl they rescued. So you won't want to miss it."

That'll keep people here, thought Morgan. She knew it wasn't unusual for volunteers to leave early—either tired of cleaning, or surrendering to the bad weather. Teenagers used the outing to sneak away from home and had friends pick them up along the main road.

Morgan wanted to go to one of the larger campgrounds farthest from Aquila Vista, so she led her friends into the first of three BLM shuttle buses. Small groups would be dropped off all along the Corridor.

Morgan resisted looking toward the back of the bus again once they'd all sat down. Lucan had yet to speak to her today. Her heart fluttered when she remembered the Valentine's Day Dance. *I thought we were finally getting somewhere.* She began humming to convince herself she didn't care. *Then again, I guess that was before I accused him of being a thief.*

The campground was near-deserted save for a lone, beat-up RV parked at the far end. Lucan was quick to suggest, "Let's split up and meet back here in an hour." The boys headed in one direction, Morgan turned in the opposite direction toward the old camper. Lawren shook her head as she and Anna followed Morgan.

Who'd be here at this time of year? Morgan wondered about the travel trailer. *It's not hunting season.* She wasn't familiar with fishing regulations. *A poacher?*

"Where are we going?" Lawren looked around uncertain.

"I just want to start at the other end of the campground," said Morgan, "away from everyone else." It wasn't a total lie. She wanted to be as far away from Lucan as he apparently wanted to be from her.

"I'm not sure this is a good idea." Anna fell behind a few steps.

Morgan knew approaching a strange campsite off-season wasn't the safest thing to do. The Pacific Northwest, with its vast forests, was a great place to disappear. But right now, as she neared the encampment, she didn't care. Empty cans, beer bottles, bottle caps, and cigarette butts were strewn all around. Wood, food wrappers, and plastic bags sat partially burned in the fire ring. *Whoever's staying here is a pig.* Next to the pit, an empty bottle of whiskey sat beside a tire that looked like it took the place of a chair. *No baby bottles, diapers, or kid's toys,* Morgan noted. *It doesn't look like a family is staying here.*

Lawren stopped several feet away. "I don't think we're supposed to pester the campers."

"I won't." Determined to find out who was squatting along the river, Morgan stood on tiptoes and looked into the dirty window of the RV's living room door. To her surprise, Anna did the same.

It wasn't much better inside. Morgan made a face. The vehicle oozed cigarette smoke, garbage, and cheap alcohol from every cracked and worn window and door seal.

"The door's been jimmied." Anna grabbed the handle and gave it a short tug. It creaked opened. "I'm going inside."

"What?" Morgan stammered, shocked. "Why?" But Anna suddenly took the lead and all Morgan could do was follow or stay outside.

"What are you guys doing?" Lawren glanced around nervous. "What if someone comes back? We'll be in trouble for sure."

Curiosity conquered uncertainty. Morgan waved over her shoulder at her friend. "We won't be long." She wasn't sure what they were looking for, but it seemed no one was home. *Thank goodness.* She looked around but didn't see anything leading to a clue as to who might be living there. No photos or mail. The green carpet was shabby, worn down to the backing in places. None of the furniture matched. *This guy shops at the dump.*

The yellowed linoleum counter was littered with maps and brochures, and an old notebook. Morgan fingered through a Molalla's *Cemetery Guide,* as well as literature from the historical society, the wildlife center, and several churches in and around Molalla.

In the margin of the wildlife center brochure she recognized Pastor Michael's handwriting. C.S.—Lucan, 12/14 8:30. *I'm pretty sure that's the day Lucan was brought to the wildlife center to start his community service!* Morgan recalled. *What's it doing here?*

She picked up the December issue of the local newspaper which lay folded to the story of the Christmas Bazaar. "This guy doesn't throw away anything." Morgan smirked at Paige and her friends, who had posed dramatically for the article's large photo. They were holding the crystal tree topper. Morgan blinked as she got her first good look at the object that had drawn her attention at the fair. *So that's what it looks like.*

A cold shiver crept down her spine. She stared at the newspaper more closely to something she hadn't noticed before. A sulky Anna could be seen standing behind the taller girls; Lucan was half hidden behind the tree. Morgan felt a little nauseous as her vision blurred. She saw vague hands wrap a box in a jacket. Heart racing, she watched as the box was stuffed into a large blue backpack.

Lawren coughed outside, pulling Morgan from her vision. She caught the edge of the counter to steady herself.

Anna picked up the notebook and rifled through its yellowed pages.

The trailer was stifling. Morgan wanted out. "He's just a tourist," she said. The atmosphere inside the vehicle was one of desperation. Morgan imagined someone who'd recently lost his job, his home, and possibly his family, with nowhere else to go. He probably just picked up the marked brochure by accident while looking for places to sightsee, and grabbed the newspaper out of some trash can. *And, here I am just being nosey.* "Let's get out of here."

But Anna didn't seem to hear her. Preoccupied, she walked a few steps down the hallway.

Morgan followed, wondering what had caught the girl's interest. They peeked into a small bedroom and bathroom with just more of the same—a dirty mattress lying on the floor, clothes flung everywhere, stains on the walls, carpeting, and sink. "This place is creeping me out," Morgan shivered. "Come on."

A pale Anna nodded and followed her back out to the campground. *The stench is probably getting to her too,* thought Morgan. *I've certainly had enough.*

While they were inside, Lawren had been busy picking up trash around the campsite, trying to look inconspicuous while playing the lookout. Morgan popped open one of her yellow garbage bags, determined to catch up with her diligent friend. *Maybe the guy will be so surprised at how nice this place looks he won't notice we snuck inside.*

Anna did the same, but Morgan noticed she stayed near the borders of the campground, as if ready to make a quick get-away. The 11-year-old's face looked strained. She didn't say a word while they finished collecting garbage.

In no time their bags were full. Morgan twisted her sack closed and looked around satisfied. "Let's get out of here before whoever lives here gets back."

They met Lucan, Zane, and Thano at the side of the road. Each of them had filled at least one bag of garbage. Thano smiled at Lawren. "We were wondering where you'd gone off to."

Zane was considerably less interested. "I'm hungry."

It wasn't long before the shuttle picked them up and headed back to Aquila Vista. Morgan's mom met them there during lunch. She put the medium dog crate she was carrying on one of the empty picnic tables and greeted Tommy. He introduced her to the group, and it got very quiet. *Young and old, people are always fascinated with owls,* Morgan knew.

"While the robin is the herald of spring," her mom began, "it's the owl that is actually the earliest nester." Morgan grinned. *Mom always starts with the facts.*

The wildlife veterinarian held up a chart showing the fourteen owls native to Oregon: the barn owl, the flammulated owl, the western screech owl, the great horned owl, the snowy owl, the northern pigmy owl, the burrowing owl, the spotted owl, the barred owl, the great gray owl, the long- and short-eared owls, the boreal owl, and the northern saw-whet owl. For about a half hour, her mother talked about owls and what made them special.

Morgan sniffed the air and scrunched her nose. "You stink." Anna was sitting next to her. Too close. She reeked of cigarettes.

"We just spent the morning picking up garbage." Anna was defensive. "We *all* stink."

Morgan's expression was deliberately probing. "Not *that* bad."

Anna looked at her self-consciously, then reached under her coat.

Morgan's eyes widened. The corner of the old notebook from the RV poked out of the girl's jacket. They looked around, but everyone seemed too interested in the lecture to notice them. Grateful her mom could hold an audience's interest, Morgan grabbed Anna's sleeve and the girls slid down the bench as far away from the crowd as they could. "You stole the book from the camper!"

"I didn't steal it." Anna's face was defiant as she slipped the book back under her coat. "I stole it *back*. This is my great-grandmother's journal."

Morgan was flummoxed. "What's your great-grandmother's journal doing in that beat up old trailer?"

"I don't know. But it has her name on it."

"Today we're going to release a great horned owl that was brought to the wildlife sanctuary in October last year." The girls sat in silence as Morgan's mom explained how the first-year bird had been unable to establish her own territory before winter. "Female raptors are larger than males but, despite her size, she was driven from one occupied territory to another. Eventually she was found, starving," she said.

Morgan emptied her lunch bag, pulled out a zip-lock baggie, and handed it to Anna. "Put it in here, or we'll get caught for sure." She hoped the air-tight seal would cut down on the overwhelming smell, especially on the bus ride back to school.

"Spring is the time for new beginnings." Mom finished the lecture on the up-beat, something the musically inclined Morgan was familiar with. And, of course, she had most of the lectures memorized. "It's the beginning of abundance, and an ideal time to let this bird try again."

A few of the group cheered before her mom could hush them. The bird clattered in the box. She carried the crate a little distance away, set it down, and opened the door. Unable to spread its broad wings, the large, mottled gray-brown owl walked out of the crate. It swiveled its rounded head and stared at them with large, glowing yellow eyes. Feather tufts over its ears resembled horns. The bird growled at them, *krrrrooooo,* sounding every bit the 'flying tiger' that was its reputation. It spread its wings and lifted off, disappearing into the nearby trees to several "ooos" and "ahhhs." The owl was starting its second chance at life.

Pushing back thoughts about the mysterious journal for now, Morgan searched for Lucan. He was leaning against one of the log posts that held up the structure's roof.

Spring is the time for new beginnings. The thought echoed in Morgan's mind as she looked at Lucan. *There's good and bad in everyone.*

Morgan resolved to make things right between them. After all, she didn't *know* that he had stolen anything. She sighed. She really liked the person she'd gone to the Valentine's Day dance with. Maybe she could get to know *that* guy better.

* * * * *

Morgan reached inside the plastic animal crate and pulled out a baby raccoon. The three animals remaining inside squirmed to close the space between them. Their eyes were still sealed shut, almost hidden by their distinctive black masks. They were no more than three weeks old. She handed the kit to Lucan. "These are kidnap victims. A neighbor trapped and got rid of the mother and brought the babies to us."

Her mom cleared her throat and gave her daughter a warning stare. "Unintentional kidnapping, for all we know, dear."

The raccoons were quiet and cool to the touch — very unlike raccoons. "Someone dropped these off at the door before we got here this morning," she continued, grabbing one of the warmed baby bottles of formula from the table. Morgan offered it to the raccoon, but the kit refused the nipple. "They might not be feeling too well yet," she said, concerned. "They got chilled outside. We put them on a heating pad right away, but it might take a while."

Lucan wrapped his hands around the animal and blew his warm breath on it, offering as much heat as he could.

Morgan rubbed the rubber nipple of the bottle against her raccoon's mouth. "At least they don't look starved." She squeezed the plastic bottle until a drop of milk leaked out. The whitish liquid dribbled down the kit's chin and was soaked up by the towel on Morgan's lap. She looked to her mom for advice.

Mom checked off the list of animals on the treatment board one-by-one as she finished administering any medications. "They don't thermo-regulate very well at this age. They're not hungry because their metabolisms have slowed way down." She smiled at the kids reassuringly. "Not to worry. Within a couple of hours they'll be crawling around, screaming for food."

"I phoned your mother," Mom said to Lucan. "We thought it might be a good experience for you to take care of these babies, if you're willing."

He hesitated. "I've never even raised a puppy or kitten. I wouldn't know how." He stroked the raccoon kit gently.

Morgan watched baby animal magic weave its slow, clandestine way in. She grinned. "It's easy. And fun. I can show you how. I raise orphans every year — raccoon, opossum. I even fostered a beaver once."

"Wait a minute," Mom cautioned. "It's a big responsibility. Lucan needs time to think about it."

"*I know.*" Morgan dragged the admission into a long sigh. "They have to be raised at home."

Mom looked at Lucan. "Fostering is *not* easy, especially when they're very young. For a while, you'll have to feed them every couple of hours 'round-the-clock."

Lucan gulped. "You mean day and night?" He looked at the two raccoons still in the crate waiting to be fed.

Mom nodded. "Your mother said she'll take care of them while you're at school, but you have to be responsible for them the rest of the time. You'll have them for several months until they're weaned. And your schoolwork *can't suffer.*"

"Come on." Morgan prodded. "They grow up *really* fast. In just a few weeks you'll only have to get up once during the night. Raccoons are a kick. You'll see. It'll be a blast."

The raccoon in Lucan's lap stirred, responding to the boy's warmth. It chirred as it started to poke around, looking for food. Morgan's raccoon squirmed, responding to its sibling. She smiled, offering it a bottle. The kit opened its mouth and soon both animals were sucking milk with enthusiasm.

"They really seem to like this stuff," said Lucan. "What's in it? It doesn't smell like milk."

"Condensed milk, water, egg yolk, vitamins, and a touch of Karo syrup to sweeten it." Morgan grinned. "You'll have the formula memorized in no time. You have to make it fresh every day."

Lucan's raccoon sneezed milk out its nostrils and coughed. He pulled the bottle away and dabbed the animal's mouth and nose with the towel on his lap. He looked at Morgan uncertainly.

"Raccoon tongues are broad and flat." Morgan repositioned her kit so it was more upright. "You'll have to figure out which position is best for each of them so they don't inhale the milk."

Lucan rearranged the baby several times before it managed to drink without coughing. It paddled all four legs to push itself closer and, at the same time, to push any competitors out of the way. Lucan smiled crookedly. "This might be fun."

Morgan grabbed toilet paper from the table and began to softly wipe her raccoon's bottom while it nursed. It eliminated.

"Or *not*." Lucan pulled a face before reluctantly doing the same with a huge wad of TP so as to keep his fingers far away from the sticky goo.

It didn't take long before the baby raccoons were full and happy, and curled up once again on the heating pad. Lucan took the four of them home with him at the end of his shift.

* * * * *

"The Spring Equinox and Easter are close together this year." Morgan plopped a paper grocery bag on the desk. It was the third week of March. Lucan sat on the reception room couch feeding one of his raccoons. His eyes carried heavy shadows from lack of sleep. Getting up at night to care for them was taking its toll. She hadn't seen him much outside of school since he'd started fostering the kits, which kept him at home and away from the wildlife center. "That'll make things easier," she said.

"What things?" Lucan interrupted her meandering thoughts. He finished feeding and returned the last of the four raccoons to the crate. Morgan watched him walk to the kitchen and hand Jackie the bottles for cleaning. He washed his hands in the kitchen sink as Morgan's aunt scrubbed the bottles with a round brush, then stood them open-end down in the drying rack with the rest of the clean dishes.

"Celebrating, of course." Morgan was bright, trying to infect him with her passion. She was still hoping to make things right between them. "We get ready for Easter and, at the same time, honor Ostara."

"The wildlife center hosts an annual Easter Egg hunt," Jackie explained, wiping her hands on a clean towel. "And we usually have a good turn-out, so it takes a bit of preparation."

Lucan scowled. "Sounds like more work."

"The Spring Equinox, or Ostara, from the German word Eostre, usually falls *before* Easter, so we prepare what we can then." Jackie shrugged. "It's a good way to get a jump on things *and* remind ourselves to stay balanced as life starts to get more hectic."

"You and I get to fill plastic eggs with candy today." Morgan pulled a bag each of chocolate eggs, oval malt balls, and brightly colored jellybeans from her paper shopping bag. She loved the springtime, when everything was bursting with new energy. "Lawren's coming by to help us create treasure maps of our Nature Trail for the kids to follow."

"We're going to hide them *today*?" Lucan blinked. "It's dark. And it's raining outside." His eyes clouded over. "It's always raining."

Morgan realized she still knew very little about him. *Wherever he came from, it's obviously drier than it is here in Oregon.*

"No, silly." Morgan refused to let his grumpiness dampen her enthusiasm. "The maps will help us hide the eggs quickly on Easter morning and keep track of any that aren't found."

"We'll also paint a few eggs today." Jackie pulled the box of painting supplies from the hallway closet. "I like hard-boiled eggs, and so do the raccoons and opossums."

"So does Cyrano." Morgan enjoyed watching the center's turkey vulture slowly peel first the shell, then the white, from the egg, then eat the yolk he favored first.

"I can't remember the last time I painted eggs," said Lucan. Morgan saw Lucan's eyes wander, as if searching for a long-ago memory. But then he shot back with his customary stiff retort. "That's for kids."

"*Again* with the kid thing?" Morgan felt her resolve to be nicer to Lucan disappear. She returned fire before she could catch herself. "When did you stop being a kid?"

At that moment, Morgan didn't know who she was madder at, him or herself. *No matter how hard, I try*, she thought, *I can't seem to stop getting ticked off at him.* She searched his sober face for the guy she'd liked so much at the Valentine's Day Dance, the one who cared enough about animals to foster orphans. But all she saw was a kid who was growing up too fast.

I don't ever want to get that old, she decided, *even when I'm all grown up.* "You don't have to," she reminded him.

"It's the Equinox." Jackie cut in. "That means *equal* day and night." She returned the conversation to the weather. "It's not always dark; it just feels that way because of the overcast. Oregon can be a moody place."

"Feeling like it is as good as being it," Lucan muttered under his breath. He looked at them, defeated, and exhaled loudly. "I guess I'm just tired from being up every night with the raccoons."

Despite the reasonableness of his defense, Morgan's limited patience was already spent. "When are you going to get used to the weather?" she snapped. "It's Oregon."

"If you'd rather," said Jackie, "you guys can shovel new dirt into the animal pens." Her tone, and the threat of the unpleasant job, signaled the end of the growing dispute. She handed the box to Lucan. "Or you can help paint Easter eggs. *Together*." Her resolute gaze moved from Morgan to Lucan. "The choice is yours."

Lucan stared out the window at the weather, *as if* he were actually considering it, before taking the box from Jackie.

* * * * *

Easter morning started with Sunrise Service. Morgan was glad it was optional to observe Lent by abstaining from something she enjoyed for forty days before Easter. *I don't do deprivation,* she thought.

After church, while parishioners enjoyed coffee and cake in the rec room, Morgan's mom drove Lawren, Lucan, and Morgan to the wildlife center. They would have an hour to hide the candy-filled plastic eggs along the Nature Trail according to their treasure map.

They headed back to the clinic when they were finished. "We're lucky." Lawren said, shielding her eyes from the growing sun. "It looks like it's going to be a beautiful day. Who's the Easter Bunny this year?"

"A new guy." Morgan folded the map containing the location of all the Easter eggs and stuffed it in her back pocket so they could pick up any unfound treasure at the end of the day. "I was surprised. He doesn't seem the type."

A strange man, Derek Angst had only been volunteering at the wildlife center a few months, and he seemed afraid even of their permanent residents, who were accustomed to, and kinder to, their human caregivers than the wild ones. "He avoids the animals whenever possible," said Morgan, "and is squeamish when it comes to preparing their food."

"Most people come to the sanctuary to work *with* the animals," said Lawren. "But I get that cutting up mouse and rat carcasses could make someone squeamish."

"Yeah, it's hard to get them to do any of the million other jobs that need doing to keep the place going."

"Why is he still here?" Lucan wondered.

Morgan shrugged. "Who knows? He could just be trying to overcome his fears." They'd had volunteers who'd tried to conquer their anxiety by working at the center in the past. Sadly, they usually failed. They loved animals, but from a respectful distance.

Lawren jabbed her thumb at an oversized rabbit outfit that hung on the coat rack just inside the door. "It usually takes a bit of doing to convince someone to wear the suit," she told Lucan.

Lucan blinked at the odd looking ensemble. "Is that on purpose?"

Morgan shrugged. "It's not your typical Easter Bunny getup, but I love it." Donated years ago, the costume was likely halves of two suits—the top being your standard white rabbit, while the bottom was dark with white only on its belly and the underside of its tail—a deer, maybe?

Lucan choked down a snicker. "It's certainly memorable."

"We couldn't have planned it any better," Morgan insisted. "What better way to celebrate the Equinox as well as Easter?"

"Show's on," Lawren announced. The first cars were driving into the wildlife center's parking lot. It wasn't long before the center was full of eager kids. Dividing them into groups, Mom and Aunt Jackie, Lucan, Lawren, and Morgan led tours through the sanctuary that ended at Oliver's pen. The kids took turns petting AWF's lop-eared bunny while listening to the history, biology, and mythology of rabbits.

When the tours were complete Mom clapped her hands. "Time for the Easter egg hunt."

Morgan looked up to see their volunteer rabbit handing out plastic Easter baskets on the front lawn, waving the kids on their way to good fortune on the Nature Trail.

"Good thing we created more than one map." Lucan handed a plan to the last kid and sent him and his family out onto the Nature Trail. He looked relaxed.

Each of the maps led to the discovery of only a few eggs. "It's the only way to make sure each of the kids finds some. Otherwise, all the older kids would wipe out the treasure before the little kids could find any." Morgan was enjoying the warm spring day. She was glad for the change in Lucan. Maybe things between them were back on track.

"Entertaining kids is fun, but I wouldn't want to do it every day." They plopped on the reception room couch exhausted by the time the last car drove away around noon, but Morgan knew their day wasn't over yet. "We still have to collect any eggs that were missed." She pulled the master map from her back pocket.

"I don't mind as long as we can keep whatever we find." Lucan unwrapped a chocolate egg and popped it into his mouth. He nodded toward the mismatched bunny costume hanging back on the coat rack. "Your Easter rabbit got outta here pretty quick."

Morgan wrinkled her nose at the strong odor of cigarettes that emanated from the suit. "He certainly wasn't much help. He arrived after set-up and left before clean-up."

Lucan chuckled. "He just took advantage of the first rule of wearing a costume."

"Did you know there were rules to wearing costumes?" Lawren asked Morgan, who shrugged and shook her head.

"Sure. Especially around little kids." Lucan went on to explain. "You're not allowed to do anything that isn't child-friendly, including putting on or taking off your costume where you can be seen."

Morgan hadn't considered that. "I guess seeing a headless bunny could scar a kid for life."

Lawren sniffed and pulled a face. "I hate when a smoker wears the suit." She waved her hand in front of her face. "We're definitely going to have to give that thing a good airing."

"It could take until next Easter to get rid of that stench," said Morgan. The smell of the costume gave them the incentive they needed to head back outside. It didn't take long to pick up any litter and the few items that hadn't been found by the guests. Morgan led the way to the barn to store the plastic eggs and baskets for next year's hunt. "Holy smokes." Her eyes grew wide.

They'd barely entered the barn when they saw the lock to the storage room had been jimmied. The door was standing wide open; the contents of the room had been thrown everywhere. "Go get Mom. We've been robbed."

Lawren ran to the clinic.

"Who could have done this?" Lucan stared. "Was anything taken?"

"The center was full of people today." Morgan swallowed hard, looking at Lucan. "Anyone could have." *Anyone but him,* she thought. *He was with me.* She flushed, ashamed at all her past suspicions. *I guess this clinches it. He really is innocent.*

Morgan's mom and aunt appeared at the door. "Don't touch anything," said Jackie. "We need to call the police, and Uncle Rick." Jackie's husband was a retired county sheriff.

Mom pulled out her phone and dialed.

It would take two hours for the cops to arrive. "No emergency," they'd said. And the wildlife center was just outside the city limits, and the Molalla police's jurisdiction.

While they waited, they checked the animals. Fortunately, not one of the pens had been broken into; none of the animals had been disturbed.

Morgan's mom inventoried the contents of the storage room. "That's strange," she said. "Nothing's missing."

"Weird." Jackie shook her head. "Why would someone go through so much trouble to break in but not take anything?"

"Not that we have much to take." Rick ushered them out of the room and closed the door, nailing a board across to discourage any more trouble. "It'll cost us more to repair than they would have gotten for all the stuff in here."

Morgan held back tears. She knew the wildlife center was operating on a shoestring budget. They really couldn't afford any unnecessary bills.

When the sheriff finally arrived, all he could do was take a report. "Without any witnesses . . ." He shook his head apologetically before leaving. "We'll send a copy to your local police. They know of any vandals in the area. Maybe they can help you figure this out." He didn't sound hopeful.

"This is just like the church," Lawren whispered to Morgan.

That's right. Morgan frowned. *They were also broken into, but not robbed.* She looked at Lucan, doubt rising in her all over again. She wanted to scream at him. Demand answers. *He may not be the thief,* she thought, *but he's involved somehow. And now trouble's followed him to the wildlife center.*

"I'll call a contractor to repair the door in the morning." Mom put a reassuring arm around each of the girls and led them away from the devastation. "There's not much more we can do right now."

"We're all beat." Jackie put her gentle hand on Lucan's shoulder. "I called your mom to come get you. She should be here any minute. We can tackle clean-up tomorrow."

* * * *

"Psst. Psst."

Morgan stopped at the lunchroom door and looked around to see who might be hissing at her. She saw a secretive Anna standing just outside the large common room.

"I need your help." Anna's long reddish braid swished as she glanced furtively around to see who might notice them. First-year middle-schoolers usually kept to themselves, especially those as quiet as Anna.

"Um...hi, Anna." Morgan hadn't seen much of the girl since the river clean-up day. She'd almost forgotten about the girl's musty old family diary.

I've got my own mystery to solve. Things were really getting weird. First the Christmas tree topper was stolen. Then the church office was vandalized. And now the wildlife center storeroom was broken into. *Why?*

"I've translated my great grandmother's journal as best I can, but I still can't figure it all out, or why it was in that beat-up old trailer in the woods."

It *was* rather curious. Morgan looked into Anna's pleading eyes and forced herself to switch gears. "Translated?"

"It's in Russian."

"Huh?" Morgan hadn't considered the diary might not be in English.

"My family's originally from Russia."

Morgan blinked. "You speak Russian?"

"Not really," Anna admitted. "That's why it's taking me so long to translate." She shrugged. "What I could, that is. I couldn't ask my mom, or she'd wonder where I got the journal."

"Yeah, that would be kinda hard to explain."

"Can you meet me after school?"

Morgan considered her options. "I could ditch study break."

"*After* school in the library." Anna seemed determined not to draw any unwanted attention. She disappeared into the lunchroom, probably heading for the sixth-graders' table.

Morgan met Anna at the library after the final bell had rung and most of the other kids had cleared out. The 11-year-old pulled her great-grandmother's journal and a bright orange notebook from her backpack, ready to get to work. By now Morgan noticed the book had only the faint odor of cigarettes. *Thank goodness. Considering how bad it smelled when we found it.* "I'm surprised it aired out as well as it did."

"I worked on it in my tree house so I wouldn't get caught. It's almost as good as being outside in the fresh air." Anna searched the room for an empty table.

But the library was far from empty, or private. After-school hours gave kids a chance to study and provided a safe place for them to wait until working parents, like Morgan's mom, could pick them up.

Morgan found the out-of-the-way table Lucan had introduced her to before the Valentine's Day dance. A part of her hoped he might be there, but it sat empty in the corner. They sat down and Anna opened both her notes and the old journal. *Maybe he'll show up,* Morgan hoped.

"As far as I can tell, it's only my prababushka's diary." Anna's pretty face was marred by frustration.

Morgan raised a questioning eyebrow.

"My great-grandmother." Anna pushed her materials closer to Morgan, turning a few pages. "I don't see anything remarkable."

Morgan scanned the pages. The orange notebook contained Anna's English translation, but it looked like the girl had only managed to decipher about every third or fourth word. *We're going to be here all day.* "Can you give me the gist of it?"

Anna recounted the tale of a young Russian girl sent to America to marry a much older man.

"Gross." Morgan grimaced. "An arranged marriage."

"Apparently it was done a lot in those days. Matchmakers were paid to find wives for men who lived in places where there weren't a lot of women. Probably because life there was really hard."

"Double gross." Morgan shuddered. As if being a mail-order bride wasn't bad enough, enduring those kinds of hardships must have made Anna's great-grandmother feel like a virtual slave. "Did you know about this?"

"Sort of." Anna's blue eyes were thoughtful. "Mama told us our great-grandparents came from the old world to make a new life for themselves."

"It's not like it is now." Anna's tone became defensive. "Mama says they needed each other to survive. And most of these girls were being saved from a life of poverty."

"I guess." Morgan had a difficult time imagining there were no other options. She swallowed hard, struggling not to judge. "What happens next?"

"Shortly after their marriage, they joined a wagon-train bound for Oregon."

Morgan remembered reading about the Oregon Trail in her history class. During the 1800s the two-thousand mile trail, used first by Native Americans and then by fur traders, connected the eastern half of the continent to the west coast. "Why the Pacific Northwest?" she asked. "They could have gone south to California, where there was gold."

"I guess my praded, or great-grandfather, wanted to be a lumberjack. Which he did, and apparently he was pretty good at it. Off-season he made furniture, and even carved a bit. I think we've still got a small captain's desk he made in our attic. They did all right."

Morgan looked at the girl curiously. Most of the kids figured the Wildlings had money.

Anna answered her unasked question. "No. My family's not wealthy, at least not anymore." She went back to her translation, flipping the pages of her orange notebook to the end. "As far as I can tell, my great-grandparents fell in love and lived a happy life."

"Nothing in that says 'steal me,'" said Morgan wryly.

"That's what I can't figure out." Anna shook her head. "Why would anyone even care about this book, much less have stolen it?"

"Maybe it's all a big coincidence and they just picked it up at a junk sale." Morgan shrugged. "Or maybe they were expecting to find some of your family's wealth. Where did it all go?"

"I don't know." Anna's face reflected defeat. "I don't think my great grandmother cared about such things." She closed her notes. "I know you don't know Russian, but . . . maybe you can come up with another way to look at this."

Morgan scratched her head. Handwritten letters in a Russian alphabet would be hard to type into Google. "I'm not sure what more I can do," she admitted, "but I'll think on it.

May Day Masquerade

"The May Day Dance Committee has decided to have a Masquerade Ball this year." Dierdre, the blonde girl who had stamped Morgan's hand at the Valentine's Day Dance, counted out fliers and handed them to the first person in each row of desks. Morgan's eyes flew over the page before taking one and handing the rest stiffly to the person behind her. She avoided looking toward the back of the room so she wouldn't see Lucan. *It's a cinch he's not going to ask me to this dance. I all but accused him of stealing at the last one.*

Fostering the raccoons had kept Lucan away from the wildlife center and from Morgan. Clearly, they were nowhere near mending their relationship. In fact, they'd barely said two words to each other since the Easter break-in.

Clean-up and repairs to AWF's storage room had been quick. Even the police seemed to have put the event on the back burner. *Probably because no one was hurt and nothing was actually stolen,* Morgan guessed. She might have been able to chalk the incident up to vandals herself except for the nagging questions that continued to plague her. *Who had stolen the Christmas tree topper, and why? Who had broken into the church? Was it the same person who had raided the wildlife center? And what, if anything, did Lucan have to do with it?*

Morgan had made a few stabs at translating Anna's great-grandmother's journal without success before returning it to the disappointed sixth grader. Russian is not an easy language. Translating the old-style script using the internet was tedious and impossibly slow. She exhaled heavily, resting her head in her hand. *I'm getting nowhere fast.*

"Does that mean we *have* to come in costume?" Paige pulled Morgan out of her reverie with a bored sniff.

"I think I've got a gangster costume in a trunk somewhere." Zane sounded just a bit more interested. The class broke into excited chatter as the possibilities seemed to make the others reconsider their prospects.

"I've got a great Zombie costume." Dean stood up, stuck his arms out in front of him and staggered a few stiff steps toward the front with a vacant look in his eyes before plopping back down into his seat. The guys around him sniggered.

Morgan pushed her face into her hands. *Great! Halloween in May.*

Dierdre's crooked smile signaled a victory. Guys aren't usually too interested in dances. Fundraising is a tough business.

"We can be Bonnie and Clyde." Paige batted her eyes at Zane.

"The theme is springtime," said Dierdre. "So keep it clean, guys. No crooks, monsters, or hack-and-slash."

She's going to make a good principal someday, Morgan thought.

There was a moment of silence until one of the guys shouted, "I'm not coming as a flower!" All decorum in the classroom was lost.

Dierdre rolled her eyes while the teacher called for order. "There are suggestions on the flier," she said.

Morgan scanned the list at the bottom of the page: plants, animals, scarecrows, literary or movie characters, fairies and other magical creatures. The usual springtime assemblage.

"Any ideas?" Lawren asked from the seat next to her.

"We could come as animals." Morgan considered the possibilities. "Maybe a dragon?" She tended toward the fantastical.

"How about musical notes." Her friend grinned. "I think we can come up with something simple. And, different."

Molalla was a community of farmers and loggers, and the Oregon winters were cold and wet and long. Everyone looked forward to warmer, drier days, and celebrated the coming season with an annual Spring Fling. Sponsored by the Chamber of Commerce, crafters and local artists set up booths and tents in the local park alongside food and drink vendors. The local businesses showcased seasonal specialty items. The highlight of the annual three-day event was its two pageants — the Mother Goose Parade and the Spring Fling Cavalcade. And, of course, the middle and high school dances.

Lawren popped her hand up. "Are we going to have a Maypole again this year?" Morgan's best friend loved the traditional folk dance, performed by the elementary and middle school kids to open the festivities.

Dierdre nodded. "The Maypole will be set up in the park as usual." The high school pep squad was in charge of the age-old performance where youngsters weaved colorful ribbons while dancing around a tall pole.

"Can I stay with you again this weekend?" Lawren whispered to Morgan. The wildlife center had an information booth at the Spring Fling every year, making for a very busy weekend. It was easier for the girls to sleep-over than to get up early.

Morgan nodded. "I was afraid you'd ditch me for Thano again." She instantly regretted the snarky comment.

Lawren bit her lower lip and admitted, "We're meeting at the dance." The high school had its annual dance on Friday night; the middle school the next evening. "I hope you don't mind."

I take it back. Morgan forced a smile and shook her head. "Uh . . . no," she stammered. "I don't mind." She sighed. *I guess I'm going solo again.* She caught herself glancing back at Lucan. Her cheeks burned. He was sitting at his desk watching her. *Guys ruin everything.*

"You know, *you* can ask *him.*" Lawren didn't need to see what, or who, had flustered her best friend. "You don't have to wait for him to ask you."

"You can buy your tickets from just about anybody who's anybody." The snobby high-schooler pounded the desk for attention. "So buy them early to save your spot." Dierdre flashed a phony smile and waved as she swished toward the door. "See you all there."

The bell signaled the beginning of first period. Morgan gathered her books and clarinet, and prepared to follow Lawren to the music room. Her eyes brushed past the back wall to the door, but Lucan was already gone. Disappointment sat like a rock in the pit of her stomach.

* * * * *

The school gym was decorated with the same inexpensive streamers and balloons as every other middle school dance, Morgan noted, but instead of a simple color theme, the room was awash in painted paper flowers. Colorful garlands stretched from the center of the room to the edges, reminiscent of the Maypole. Iridescent cellophane tinsel blew in the breeze of the air conditioner vents, shimmering like rain. The dance floor was filled with costumed kids gyrating to loud music. *No wallflowers at a masquerade.*

Morgan brushed her simple white toga, which she'd chosen to wear over black tights; it was gathered at her waist with a broad leather belt of leaves and jewels. Her mom had styled her curly locks into a loose chignon held together by a double metal headband. A glittery maple leaf mask finished what she hoped was her magical look.

Morgan thought back on the relative quiet of the Valentine's Day dance as she wove her way to the refreshment table, narrowly avoiding a bumblebee buzzing around a ladybug. She raised her eyebrows at the weirdness. *People must really feel safe behind masks.* A quick scan of the room revealed little as to who was who in the mass of kids.

She looked for Lucan, shook her head and huffed. *He could be standing right next to me and I wouldn't know it.* She took a tentative bite out of her cookie, glancing casually right, then left. She almost spilled her drink when a large skunk bumped her with his hips, then raised his striped tail.

"Better watch out," Zane's eyes sparkled, throwing a look over his shoulder, "or you'll remember this day for the rest of your life." He turned his black-painted face to her, lowering the long tail that had been held up by some unseen mechanism.

Morgan grinned. A white stripe started on the boy's forehead and continued into his black wig and down his black sweatshirt. It was the wildest skunk costume Morgan had ever seen. "Great get-up. How'd you come up with that?"

"He didn't." Paige pushed between them and helped herself to punch. She wore green, her head ringed with large white petals. "Don't you recognize Flower? From Bambi." She pressed her face so close to Zane's that Morgan wondered how his black face paint didn't smudge her white petals. "I'm the daisy that got him his name." Paige smirked at her own cleverness.

Morgan raised her eyebrows, but refrained from comment. *She's a little old for Bambi, isn't she?*

"I figured if I couldn't come as a gangster," Zane shrugged, "I might as well come as a real stinker."

Paige gulped down her drink, pointed to somewhere in the middle of the dance floor, and dragged Zane into the crowd. They were quickly swallowed by the throng.

"Your costume looks amazing." Lawren materialized next to Morgan with Thano in tow. Her best friend was wearing a simple skirt that looked like the keys of a piano. A pair of glasses shaped like treble clef sat over her normal eye wear. Her boyfriend looked a little like Elton John in a weird music-military-style suit and a pair of oversized glasses.

Lawren smiled approvingly at Morgan's ensemble. "Are you the queen of the fairies?"

"Titania herself." Morgan bowed her head majestically. She scanned the room again. It was warm outside and kids were migrating in and out of the gym freely, despite all efforts by adult supervisors to keep them corralled. Morgan's aunt and uncle danced at the far end of the refreshment table. *Probably to make sure no one spikes the punch*, she thought. It was the perfect occasion to get away with just about anything; after all, no one could prove who was whom. Morgan jumped when she felt a tap on her shoulder.

"Wanna dance?" Dressed in black sweats, Lucan wore the mask of a furry bandit, complete with pointy ears and a ringed tail. His smile was relaxed.

Morgan giggled. His black and white costume looked more like the cartoon of a raccoon than the real thing, which was primarily black and tan or gray. "You're taking this raccoon thing a bit far, aren't you? She offered a shy smile and couldn't help noticing, *he's as handsome as ever.*

"It's a lot easier now that they're sleeping through the night," Lucan said. "Mom's kit-sitting so I can have the night off." He looked at her expectantly. "Well?"

"Sure." Morgan let herself be led to the dance floor. In the mob of people the room was stuffy, and they found themselves dancing much closer than she was used to. The energy in the building was palpable. A bit light-headed, Morgan looked up into Lucan's masked face, wondering for a minute what was hidden there.

I don't care. Morgan pushed any past doubts from her mind. *Not tonight.* The music changed from fast to slow and back again. She let her body find the rhythm of each song. Lucan followed, swaying and spinning, even mirroring some of her movements. One dance turned into the next, and then the next. They danced together all evening. Protected by their masks, the volume, and the anonymity of the crowd, any awkwardness quickly melted away. *I like masquerades*, thought Morgan.

"I need your help." Morgan turned reluctantly toward an anxious Paige. The girl was wringing her hands. "Zane's missing," she said.

"What's up?" asked Lawren.

Caught up in the moment, Morgan hadn't even noticed her best friend and Thano dancing nearby. "Zane's AWOL." Paige sounded genuinely concerned.

"Maybe he's gone to the restroom." Lucan let go of Morgan. "I can check for you."

"It's more than that." Paige's eyes darted to the gym door and its frazzled guards, before returning to Morgan and her friends. "Can you come?" Her tone reflected her increasing anxiety.

Lucan took Morgan's hand as the four of them followed Paige through the crowd to the exit. It wasn't hard to avoid the adult chaperones, who were busy dealing with other, less surreptitious, students.

Once in the long school hallways, they quickened their pace until they reached an open locker surrounded by Paige's three-girl crew. Zane's stuff was strewn on the floor. The tail of his skunk costume looked like it had been ripped off his black pants and lay there tattered.

Morgan picked it up and fingered the ragged edges. A dirty footprint on the white stripe indicated a person with very big feet had stepped on it, probably during a scuffle. *Mayday. Mayday. Mayday.* The age-old distress signal buzzed around in her head making her slightly nauseous. The smell of cigarettes overwhelmed her though she knew there was no smoking on school grounds. "I have a bad feeling about this." She turned to Lawren. "Go get Uncle Rick."

Lawren ran back to the gym.

After she'd disappeared, Lucan grabbed Morgan's arm and pulled her aside, whispering in her ear, "I need to show you something."

She looked at him, confused and just a bit annoyed. *What could be so important that he had to show it to me right now?* But the look on his face squelched any argument. "We'll be back in a minute," she told her friends and followed Lucan down a second, and then a third hallway.

They ended up at 'The Clothes Corner,' a school-run donation center. Morgan was floored when Lucan produced the key and unlocked the door. "How...?" she stammered.

"My mom volunteers here," Lucan told her after they'd gone inside. He flipped on a weak light, then led her through the small room to a tiny storage closet at the back of the store. It was stuffed with coats, blankets, formal wear, toys and games, etc. "They keep their best stuff in here to give away during the holidays."

At the farthest wall Lucan began to pull boxes and bags from the top shelf. He dug out a narrow wooden box. Morgan saw him hesitate. "I think they were after this," he said, and opened the box.

Morgan's chest tightened as she stared at the missing crystal star with the distinctive central heart. She recognized it from the newspaper clipping. *So I was right all along*, her mind cried. *He is the thief.* For a split second, she forgot about everything except his betrayal. "Why are you showing this to me now?"

Lucan's face was hard. "Because I think this may be the reason they took Zane."

Morgan furrowed her brows. Her mind was a jumble. Anger rose in her voice as she forced herself back into the present situation. "Who cares about a dumb old ornament?"

"I don't know," said Lucan. "But you've got to admit, a lot of strange things have been happening since it disappeared."

It didn't disappear, her mind screamed. *You took it.* She took a deep breath, trying to rein in her anger. "What's that got to do with Zane?" she spat.

"I dunno." Lucan dropped his eyes to the stolen package in his hand. "Maybe they saw us together. Maybe they got the wrong locker. Maybe they got the wrong guy."

"*They* who?"

"I don't know." Lucan dropped his eyes to the stolen package in his hand. "I admit I should've returned this dumb thing a long time ago, but . . . things just got complicated. I never found the right time."

Morgan felt the color drain from her face. The break-ins at the church and at the wildlife center — they were looking for the tree topper? Morgan snapped. "You could have told *me*. Maybe not right away, but you definitely owed it to me after they showed up at the wildlife center. They could have hurt someone. They could have hurt one of the animals."

Morgan stopped herself, unable to control the shaking. She took another deep breath. *Be reasonable*, she thought. There was no way Lucan could have known how far the crook would go to retrieve the tree topper. After all, it wasn't valuable. *Why?* Her mind buzzed trying to make sense of things. And, now they had Zane.

Lucan looked like she'd slapped him. "You think *I* took this thing?"

Morgan felt her face flush. *Is he going to lie to me again?* "Didn't you?"

"I guess I did, in a way," he admitted. "I walked off with it, even though I didn't know it."

Morgan was confused. He stole it, but he didn't?

"Someone put it in my backpack. I found it when I got home from the church after the Holiday Bazaar."

Morgan recalled her vision of the box being stuffed into a large, blue backpack. She hadn't actually seen the perpetrator. "Why didn't you tell anyone?" she asked. "Why didn't you just give it back right away?"

"I don't know why I didn't turn it in," he said. "At first I guess I was afraid to. I didn't know anyone here, after all." His eyes searched hers. "You gotta admit, it looks pretty bad," he said. "I didn't think anyone would believe me.

"Why didn't you tell me?" she demanded.

He took a deep breath to steady himself. "I'm not in a good place right now. My parents aren't happy; haven't been in for a long time." His shoulders sagged and the truth flooded out. "I wasn't sure you'd believe me, and I didn't want you to hate me."

Morgan stared at him, taken completely off guard. He'd lied to her to keep her from hating him? To protect someone? It took a minute to collect her thoughts before she could ask, "Who stole the ornament? Who put it in your pack?"

Lucan shrugged his shoulders. "That's just it, I don't know who or why. No one's come to collect it, or even ask about it."

Morgan closed the box and handed it back to Lucan. "Someone wants this thing bad enough to kidnap Zane."

Lucan stuffed everything back to the top shelf and out of sight. "I think it'll be safer to keep this thing here for now. At least until we can figure out who wants it so badly, and why."

The insidious odor of cigarettes and trash reemerged, tugging at her memory. After a minute, she said. "I think I know where they might have taken Zane."

Lucan didn't ask from where Morgan's sudden insight had materialized as he locked the door and followed her back to Zane's locker. Rick, Lawren, Thano, Paige, and her friends were waiting for them. So was Principal Johnson. And she didn't look happy.

"We need to call the police." A tear ran down Paige's face, dragging yellow paint with it. Her petals drooped sadly. Morgan had never seen the girl so frightened.

"It's probably a little soon for that." Principal Johnson was wringing her fat hands together nervously. She looked to Rick for support.

"Has anyone tried to call Zane?" asked Rick. "He might just be out with friends. He could have walked home."

Morgan was stunned. Was her uncle buying this malarkey? Principal Johnson's probably more worried about her reputation, and that of the school's, than the safety of a kid.

"I did." Paige's voice cracked. "He's not answering his cell, and he's not at home. At least not yet."

"Doesn't this spell trouble?" Morgan pointed to the locker's strewn contents and the abused costume tail.

"Not necessarily." The principal's voice wavered as she pulled out a handkerchief and mopped her face. "Why anything could have happened. This could mean absolutely nothing."

Rick pursed his lips and frowned. Her uncle looked like he was holding back a sharp retort, but then, to Morgan's surprise, he turned to them and shook his head. "She might be right. Zane could just be horsing around. He *was* dressed as a skunk."

"Just so. Just so." The principal breathed a heavy relief.

"But we should still notify the police," said Rick, "just in case."

The principal withered, out of excuses.

Rick took pictures of the scene with his cell phone, then picked up the boy's school and personal items and put them back into the locker. The lock itself was undamaged and hung open. Zane had probably unlocked it himself before being attacked. The metal clang of locker door snapping shut echoed ominously down the long hallway.

Rick put a comforting hand on Paige's shoulder. "Don't worry. I'm sure he'll turn up soon. In the meantime, you kids get back to the dance. I'll notify the police."

"I think I might know where Zane is," Morgan told her uncle when everyone but she and Lucan had been reluctantly ushered back to the gymnasium by the distraught principal. She held her breath, not sure how Rick would respond to her wild notion. She had no real evidence, after all, just a gut feeling.

"Where?" Rick asked.

"A campsite on the River Corridor."

"How would you know that?" The retired cop looked more than a little skeptical. "How *could* you?" he asked. "Unless there's something you're not telling me."

Morgan squirmed under the scrutiny. "It's just a feeling," she admitted, glad she had to explain her hunch to her uncle, and no one else. Intuition wasn't exactly grounds to send out a search party.

Rick examined her intently. For all he knew, Morgan was sending them on a wild goose chase. Then again, it wasn't like they had any real leads.

"It's not far," she said, "but we'll need to drive."

Rick rubbed the back of his neck before shrugging his shoulders and pulling out his cell phone. "I guess it won't hurt to have Jackie report this to the police while we take a quick look. I don't have better ideas at the moment."

Thirty minutes later, flashlights in hand, the trio walked the campground where the kids had picked up garbage during the RiverWatch clean-up, and where Anna had stolen back her great-grandmother's journal. Morgan looked around, disgusted. The site and fire ring they had so diligently cleared was once again covered with garbage. Worse, the beat-up RV was gone.

Morgan followed the deep tire tracks to where they had hit the main road, dragged several feet of dirt behind them on the black asphalt, and then disappeared into the darkness. "I was so sure," she said, her voice swallowed by the stillness of the night.

"It was a long shot," said Rick. He looked up and down the main drag. "There are so many campgrounds along the Corridor, they could be anywhere."

"If they're in the area at all," Lucan added quietly.

"We don't know if the person in the RV had anything to do with Zane's disappearance," said Rick. "Assuming anything's happened to Zane at all. He could be back at the dance after having a smoke under the bleachers."

But Morgan knew better. While she admitted she didn't know Zane that well, she had never seen the guy smoke or drink, or heard about him taking any drugs. She couldn't imagine the responsible student and athlete vanishing without at least telling someone.

A twig snapped, making everyone jump. Three flashlight beams shot in the direction of the disturbance. Morgan caught her breath, glad her uncle usually carried his badge and gun. With no street lights, the forest was pitch dark, and just a little bit scary.

"Grrrrrrr." Their light streams trained on a startled raccoon, scrounging through the trash for a meal. It stood on hind legs, trying to make itself appear larger than life. The animal's eyes glowed fiercely as they reflected their beams.

They jumped again as Rick's phone broke the silence. When he finished the call he looked visibly relieved, and maybe a little annoyed. "The cops searched the school and found Zane tied to the football field's goal post, drunk and smelling like an ashtray." The trio headed back to the car. "He's spinning some giant tale of being kidnapped, but he's fine." Rick yanked open the car door. "They think he probably just got punked and is trying to weasel his way out of trouble."

They drove back to the middle school in silence. Morgan thoughts were a jumble, and she couldn't get rid of the nagging feeling that she was right. *Zane was kidnapped by whoever lives in that RV. I'm sure of it. And I bet it was for that tree topper.* But they were missing something. *Why would anyone even* want *that cheap piece of junk, much less be willing to commit burglary or kidnap someone for it?*

Morgan stared out into the black night. She was glad no one had come to any harm, but she stung from Lucan's deception. *I need to take a closer look at that crystal star.* She glanced at the boy seated next to her. Lucan looked as if he had once again retreated behind his mask. But, if he was to be believed, the actual bandit was, in fact, someone else.

* * * * *

"It's like the kidnapping never happened." Lawren plopped the daily newspaper on the library table in front of Morgan, who closed the Mother's Day card she was working on and stuffed it and her colored pencils into her backpack. "And Zane swears a man in a black ski mask snatched him from behind just after he opened his locker, tied and gagged him, and dragged him to stinky parts unknown."

Morgan scanned the page six article as Lawren pulled out the chair next to her and sat down. *Kidnapping Attributed to Teenage Prank* claimed the inconspicuous headline. None of the stories circulating around the school had found their way into the report; clearly the reporter had only talked to school administrators who had done their best to cover it up. Morgan tossed the newspaper aside. "They're basically calling Zane a liar."

"And a drunk." Lawren scoffed. "As if Zane would ever drink or smoke. He says he was forced to drink the alcohol."

"Probably because they wanted to make him forget," said Morgan. "Or at least be hazy on the details."

"Or make sure no one believes him." Lawren was clearly outraged. "But I do."

"So do I," said Morgan. "Zane is a good student, and is one of the school's top jocks. If they don't listen to *him* . . ." Principal Johnson had clearly done a good job whitewashing the story. Even the few quotes by Zane's parents sounded scripted. *They were happy for his safe return and would take appropriate disciplinary measures.*

They probably threatened his position on the football team if they didn't cooperate. Morgan snapped the newspaper shut in disgust. The first page was dominated by photos of the Spring Fling, including a large picture of the center's turkey vulture. *Cyrano makes a guest appearance at Spring Fling,* read the caption.

"Can I talk to you?" Anna's soft voice interrupted them.

Morgan bit her lip and reluctantly faced the sixth-grader. "Uh . . . sure." She hadn't talked much to the quiet girl since the spring river clean-up, and had almost forgotten about her great-grandmother's journal.

Anna slid into a chair across the table. Nervous eyes darted from Morgan to Lawren and back.

Lawren took the hint, and got up to leave. "I guess I'll see you later."

"How's the translating coming?" Morgan asked Anna after Lawren had gone.

"I haven't managed to get much farther. I was hoping you might have come up with another way to tackle the problem." She looked at Morgan expectantly.

Morgan wracked her brain. So much had happened in the last month, she honestly hadn't given the journal much thought. They sat for a while staring at the open book before Morgan finally had an idea. "Instead of trying to translate the thing word-for-word, why don't we come up with a list of words to look for?"

"It might be faster."

For the next half-hour they created a list of words that might catch the attention of a thief — gold, silver, treasure, fortune, secret, jewels, map, hidden, diamonds, and the like.

Morgan put down her pencil and stretched her fingers when coming up with a new word of interest became painfully slow. "This will at least give us something to start with. Why don't you let me take the journal home and stare at it for a while? I'll use the internet to translate these terms into Russian, and then look through the book to see if I can find any mention of them."

Anna's smile was relieved as she slid the journal and notebook toward Morgan. "Thanks. To tell you the truth, I'm kinda sick of studying this thing. It could use a fresh pair of eyes."

But Morgan's attention was pulled away from Anna when she spotted Lucan sitting at a corner table. *He must've come in while we were working*, she thought.

"No problem." Morgan forced her attention back to their project, smiling weakly. She stuffed Anna's journal into her backpack fully intending to follow the girl out of the library, but something compelled her to stay. She grabbed the newspaper and flipped through it after Anna had gone. Most of the weekly rag was dedicated to the Spring Fling and the parades. She skimmed the articles and searched the photographs, not sure what she was looking for.

And then it caught her attention. In the background of one of the photos stood two smiling boys, both in black-and-white costumes. Her eyes flew open. She folded the paper, grabbed her stuff, and hastened to Lucan's table. "I know why Zane was kidnapped," she told him stiffly, dropping the paper in front of him and pointing to the picture. "You were right. They were looking for you." And she was sure the culprit was the cigarette smoking alcoholic in the beat-up RV, whoever *that* was.

* * * * *

"Of course," Morgan stared in disbelief at Christmas tree topper sitting in its protective wooden box. She looked up at Lucan in the dim light of the Clothes Corner closet. Deep shadows exaggerated his sober expression. "Hidden in plain sight," she nodded, glancing around at all the junk collected over the years and stashed forgotten in the back of the small storage room.

The ornament was heavier than she had expected. *Probably because it's real crystal*, Morgan guessed, *instead of light-weight plastic*. She tilted the box so the ornament caught what light it could. The multifaceted star glinted even in the weak lighting. In the center of the decoration, an opaque red heart guarded its secret closely.

She couldn't keep a reluctant note of admiration from her voice when she looked back at Lucan's face. "It's the perfect place. Why didn't I think of it?"

Lucan shrugged. "I figured no one would find it buried under all that stuff."

Silence stretched between them.

When he finally spoke, his voice had an edge. "I don't know why I didn't just turn it over. I certainly didn't think it was going to be this big a deal. It's just a stupid tree topper. It can't be worth anything."

"You don't know that," she sighed. "Just because it's donated."

Lucan stared at the crystal, furrowing his brow. The distance between them was as great as ever, even now she knew he wasn't the thief.

But Morgan needed more of an explanation. "You said you weren't in a good place right now," she said quietly, not sure he was ready to talk to her. "What did you mean by that?"

"I don't know." Lucan's eyes were as cold as ice. "I guess I just got mad."

"Mad?" Morgan struggled to understand. It explained the "bad attitude" that had brought him to the wildlife center. "Who or what are you so pissed off at that you'd let everyone think you stole *anything*, then lied about it? Even me!"

He snatched the box from her and slammed the lid shut. "I think my mom and dad are getting a divorce."

Morgan caught her breath. Over the years several of her friends had lived through the divorce of their parents. Some were okay with it, glad for an end to the fighting. For others, it blew apart their lives. A few had even been forced to move away to be with other family. It explained his bad attitude, and the acting out.

"I don't expect you to understand," Lucan retorted.

Morgan thought back to the Valentine's Dance. *I'm glad it's just me and Mom*, she'd told him. She could kick herself now. She hadn't thought much about her revelation at the time. Practically everyone knew Morgan had only one parent, though maybe not why. And she was okay with that, accustomed to having no father. Every family is different, her mother had taught her. Lucan looked close to tears. She couldn't imagine separating from someone you loved. She bit her lip, *no wonder he couldn't talk to me, even lied*.

Refocusing, she took the box back. "We need to get this someplace where we can take a good look at it," she said. *It needs to go back to the church,* she thought, *but not before I find out why the ornament is so important. And to whom.*

"Where?" Lucan took a deep breath and exhaled slowly. He seemed relieved his secret was finally out.

"The wildlife center." Morgan headed for the door. "It'll be safe there. Whoever is interested in this thing has *already* searched there."

Summer Wishes

"This is a really cool Memorial Day project." Lawren tried to coax Morgan into a better mood as she followed her friend away from the rest of their classmates to a more remote, and rundown, section of the cemetery. Each of the kids carried several sheets of art paper and a charcoal stick. Lawren shivered, not entirely from the cold. Her eyes warily scanned the grounds. It didn't look so intimidating in the bright light of the late May morning. "I've got to admit, living near a graveyard gives me the creeps," she said, "so I pretty much avoid it." The Pioneer Cemetery bordered the tiny Lutheran church where her mother pastored.

Morgan walked slowly past each of the gravestones casually reading epitaphs, trying to decide which might be interesting enough to warrant a shadow drawing. Some were upright blocks decorated with statues of angels, others were merely markers. Many had only a name and dates of birth and death etched deeply in plain stone. A few had interesting remarks on the life of the person or persons buried there.

"*Wait for me my dear, the best is yet to be.*" "*Here lies the body of a stranger. Worry not, God knows you.*" And the almost desperate, "*I was somebody.*" Morgan smirked at the really old and barely readable, "*At home and in their beds, a thief *broke in and killed them dead."* And Morgan's favorite, *"A dedicated teacher for who school is finally out."*

"What's with you?" Lawren questioned insistently. She seemed determined to annoy Morgan out of her silent reverie. "You've been brooding and distant for the last couple of weeks now. I've tried to give you your space, but this is just not like you. Spill."

"I've had a lot on my mind." For some reason, Morgan hadn't been able to tell her best friend about either Anna's journal or the Christmas tree topper, and how Lucan had inadvertently stolen it from the church. She hadn't told anyone. Keeping secrets from Lawren weighed heavily on her. All she'd managed was to find a good spot at the wildlife center to hide the ornament and try to forget Lucan's remoteness. But she knew she couldn't let it go for long. Not if someone was looking for it. *Given the kidnapping, who knows what lengths they'd go to get it?*

Morgan stopped at a grave that particularly caught her attention. Instead of the customary angel guardian, a carved stag topped a large, square monument. *That must've cost the family plenty*, she thought. Most of the inhabitants of the small town, past and present, were generally quite poor. She read the inscription.

She was as dear as life could be
came alone across the sea
to live her life along with me.

Anna Olen Wildling
Josef Wildling

The message was haunting, and the deer reminded Morgan of her Yule vision quest with Lucan. *Everything reminds me of Lucan*, she chided herself. She wondered if the hurt would ever go away. She handed Lawren her extra supplies before laying a sheet of paper over the rough carved stone and wiping the soft charcoal over the imprint.

"I was going to copy that stone." Anna's soft voice interrupted them before Morgan had only finished half her drawing. "That's my great-grandparent's grave."

Morgan's hands froze without lifting her charcoal. "This is your great-grandmother?" *Is this the woman that wrote the journal?* she wondered.

"Really?" Lawren moved to get a better view of the marker. "I didn't know you had family buried here?"

"My family has been in Oregon a long time." The Wildlings were one of the founding families in Molalla. Lumber had made the family wealthy at one time, although it didn't look like much of any fortune remained.

"I don't think it matters if we work on the same stones." Morgan broadened her strokes so she could finish faster. "There are only a few really cool ones."

But she felt guilty. She hadn't exactly sought out Anna since taking her great-grandmother's journal. She reread the epitaph, seeing it in a new light. *Was this the same woman who'd come to America as a mail-order bride. The journal said her great-grandparents' lives had become a real-life love story.*

"I knew I'd find you here, my little Anoushka."

Morgan gasped at the endearment she vaguely remembered from a daydream. She looked up at the stocky woman wearing a pale yellow, floor-length dress and a white scarf on her head. A few red curly strands had escaped to dance in the breeze. Their art teacher, Anna's mother, was making the rounds, checking on the whereabouts and progress of her students. The woman touched the stone lovingly. "Great-grandfather was never the same after she died." She smoothed her daughter's curly hair.

Morgan turned to re-examine the bottom of the gravestone. Anna's great-grandfather had died over fifteen years *after* her great-grandmother; practically a lifetime alone.

Anna's face was sad, and a little sullen. "I miss grandma. I'm going to do her grave after I finish this one."

Her grandmother is buried here too? Morgan knew few people were considered founding pioneers, and they were the only ones allowed to be laid to rest in this cemetery.

"I know you are angry at me," Mrs. Wildling pulled a handkerchief from her pocket to dab her eyes, "but, honestly, you will never forget her. In time it will get easier."

Morgan fidgeted and glanced at Lawren, who shrugged her shoulders subtly.

"Anna is upset that we gave away her grandmother's belongings," Mrs. Wildling explained.

"Did you have to do it so soon, Mama?"

"It was time enough, little one, and there are others who need them far more than we do." Her mother's entreat fell on deaf ears. She shook her head as she moved on.

"We need to get together to go over your diary." Morgan hoped to make Anna feel better. "I've looked up all the words I can think of and added them to what you've translated. Maybe it'll make more sense to you now."

Anna relaxed and offered a soft smile. "I thought you'd forgotten."

"I've just been busy." They set a time to get together. Anna finished her rubbing, then moved on to her grandmother's gravestone.

Lawren folded her arms as well as her full hands would allow and looked at Morgan expectantly. "What diary?"

"We've got some catching up to do." Morgan knew she needed help. She told Lawren everything—about the crystal ornament, the diary, the stranger in the RV, the break-ins. Even Lucan's confession. "It's time to get to the bottom of this, and I'm going to need any help I can get."

A glint caught Morgan's eye. She looked around the graveyard. It was a gloomy place even in the daytime. And then she saw it again, a sparkle in the sunlight, like the wings of a fairy. A peacock green dragonfly sat on the Wildling tombstone.

"Oooohhh, that's good luck, isn't it?" Lawren asked.

The dragonfly took off, gliding towards them on clear iridescent wings. It landed on Morgan's shoulder, attracted to her pale blonde hair.

"What's it telling you?"

"I'm not sure," Morgan barely whispered, not wanting to scare off the insect.

Long, slender wings opened and closed slowly. *Things are about to change.*

The girls watched for a while, before it finally took off and disappeared. Morgan smiled. The place didn't seem quite as forlorn, her mood not as heavy. Maybe it was coming clean with her best friend. Or, maybe it was a touch of dragonfly magic.

* * * * *

"What are you working on?" Mom looked up from her patient records. She was still dressed in her surgical scrubs, having just finished a long procedure to repair the broken wing of a red-tailed hawk.

She keeps track of what I'm doing more than any of my friends' moms do, Morgan grumbled to herself. She knew better than to complain out loud.

"History homework," she reported. *It's not a total lie.* She, Lawren, and Lucan, were sitting with Anna at the wildlife center trying to make sense out of the girl's great-grandmother's diary.

"Anything interesting?" Mom prodded for details.

"The lives of some of the early settlers in Molalla." Lawren smiled innocently. The daughter of a Lutheran minister and a trial lawyer, she'd learned to play the evasion game as well as anyone, and better than most.

Lucan was quiet. He'd withdrawn again since his May Day revelation.

To Morgan's relief, Mom's phone interrupted the inquisition. They lowered their voices, even though she knew Mom's work would keep her attention away from anything they might say.

"Can anyone make any sense of this yet?" Morgan flipped a few pages of the handwritten journal. It was in surprisingly good shape for its age. Although some of the words had faded almost to obscurity, much of the writing was clear and legible. If you knew Russian.

Anna's pencil beat an annoying rhythm onto the desk as she stared at her binder. "I've converted as much as I can into English. My Russian sucks."

Glad her mother hadn't heard the curse, Morgan looked up a few more guess-words on the internet and added them to Anna's translation, but there still wasn't enough to make any sense of it. She plopped down her own pencil exasperated. "That still leaves a lot of gobbledygook."

The foursome stared frustrated at the pages. An insect buzzed too close to Morgan's ear. She thought on the dragonfly — *change*. Change your perspective. "We need to look at this from a different angle." She paused, not wanting to bring up a sore subject for Anna, but it couldn't be helped. "You said your grandmother died a while back, right?"

Anna nodded, not sure where Morgan was heading.

"What did your mom do with her stuff?"

"Gave it away, mostly."

"Where?"

Anna and Lawren answered in chorus. "The church."

"What's *that* got to do with anything?" asked Lucan.

"I've got a hunch." Morgan knew they needed to switch things up. And, she needed to pull the group together to solve the mystery of the old diary and the Christmas tree topper which, at this point, she believed might be connected. She got up and looked over Lucan's shoulder to the computer screen. "Look up the Russian words for 'sacred' and 'heart'."

Lucan did as he was told, copying the foreign words onto scraps of paper and handing it to Anna. Her face paled and she looked at each of her companions' questioning face before dropping her eyes to her great-grandmother's journal. She pointed to an obscure word on one of the faded pages. It could easily have been missed.

"The Christmas tree topper belonged to my great-grandmother? How did you know?" she almost shouted.

"A dragonfly told me." Morgan shrugged. "The ornament is made from cut glass, not plastic, so I figured it was old. It's stored in a wooden box, so it must be important . . . at least to someone."

"*You* didn't know?" Lawren looked quizzically at Anna.

She shook her head and inhaled slowly before speaking. "The tree topper belonged to my grandma," she admitted. "She must've got it from my great-grandmother. She kept tons of old junk in the attic."

Realization hit both Lucan and Morgan at the same time.

"You're the one who stole the ornament!" Morgan exclaimed. She should have suspected Anna when the girl was so willing to break in and steal the journal from the RV. *The girl's a regular klepto; or a master thief in the making.*

"And put it in *my* bag." Lucan exclaimed.

"That was an accident." Anna tugged nervously on a red curl. "I thought it was my bag. I was in a hurry, and they look a lot alike — both big and blue."

Morgan had a sudden realization. *That's why the totem stag had chosen Lucan!* By hiding the ornament inside Lucan's backpack, Anna had inadvertently pulled him into her family's history, a story that had begun generations ago at that log cabin.

"Why didn't you ask me for it?" Lucan wondered.

"At first I didn't know who had it." Anna looked like she might cry. "Then after you got into so much trouble I was afraid to."

"But that stuff was donated to the church," said Lucan. "Why would your parents do that if it's valuable?"

"Happens all the time," said Morgan. "The trick is to spot the good stuff buried in all the junk you get." Sorting through wildlife center donations to separate the trash from the useable had become one of Morgan's jobs — stuff they could repair, stuff they could use, and stuff they could sell for a little extra money.

Anna's eyes lowered. "Although my family was well off at one time, we're not anymore. Nobody thought that stuff was worth anything. Except to me."

"Somebody thinks it's worth something," said Morgan. "And we need to figure out why."

Lucan combined the words and typed "Sacred Heart Christmas tree topper" into the computer's search engine. It pulled up several styles of the crystal ornament, both antique and modern. As far as they could tell, it was a common Russian holiday trim, not particularly valuable despite its age.

"Nope. Nothing special," said Lawren.

Morgan heaved a sigh. "Certainly not worth the trouble someone seems to be going through to track it down."

Mom's office chair creaked as she hung up her phone and stood up. "I've got to go to the high school," she said, and slipped her purse over her shoulder heading for the door. "There's an injured fawn sitting along the track. I don't know how bad it's hurt so I'm going to pick it up myself instead of sending a volunteer."

"We'll be fine." Morgan was used to being alone at the wildlife center while Mom gallivanted all over the county rescuing animals.

"We need to take another look at that topper," Morgan told her friends after her mother had gone. She went to the fridge and grabbed some grapes before leading the way to the Nature Trail.

"*That's* where you hid the crystal?" Lucan stared into Jerome's pen in horror. The skunk poked his head sleepily from the lower level of his elaborate two-story home, sniffing for treats.

"The volunteer who made his condo didn't realize that striped skunks are ground dwellers. Jerome never uses the second level." Morgan shrugged her shoulders. "It's the perfect place to hide things." She unlocked the pen door, being careful not to squish the soft fruit in her hand — bribery for the enclosure's occupant. "I figured nobody would look there."

"If they did, they'd be hard pressed to get it." Lawren stepped back from the pen, keeping a healthy distance between her and the animal. Anna didn't need any convincing to do the same.

Morgan snickered. Her friends couldn't stand far enough away. An intact skunk can scent bomb for up to ten feet, and the fumes can travel a whole lot farther than that. "Hmpf," she chuckled. "He can't hurt anyone. He's been descented."

Morgan dropped the hook into the metal eye, latching herself inside the pen. She approached the miniature structure that was the animal's den slowly so as not to surprise the skunk. *He's cranky when he's half-awake*, she thought, *and not beyond a nip*. Jerome now stuck half-way out of the doorway.

"Maybe *he* can't," Lucan craned his neck to the side to see around Morgan and past Jerome, "but Sasha can." The wild skunk was curled up in a hollow under the den, visible below the buried chain link flooring that was the only thing separating the female from her captive mate.

"Relax, his girlfriend knows we're not going to hurt either of them," Morgan assured them. Just the same, she kept her voice low and made no sudden movements. *It doesn't pay to surprise a skunk, no matter how accustomed to humans they are.* It was a thought she kept to herself. "Besides, she's probably sound asleep." Nonetheless, Morgan sent peaceful thoughts toward the animals while, at the same time, regulating her own breath and heartbeat to broadcast calm.

"*Probably?*" Lucan's whisper was skeptical.

Rather than hand Jerome one grape at a time, like she usually did, Morgan dropped the whole handful in front of him, hoping to keep him busy while she reached into the entryway and snaked her arm up through a cutout between the levels to the second story. It took a minute or so to wrap her fingers around the box containing the Christmas tree topper. "Drat," she hissed. Apparently Jerome had been nosey enough to move the box from its easy-access spot. She couldn't pull it out without some clatter.

Sasha stirred and lifted her head sleepily; black eyes looked directly at Morgan.

Morgan froze and cooed softly to the drowsy animal. "Easy girl, I'm not here to hurt you. I just want this box." When Sasha didn't move, Morgan continued to slowly pull the container through the hole and out the entry. Jerome munched, peacefully ignoring them, but Sasha tucked her feet underneath herself, ready to dart out of her underground dwelling.

Morgan's friends took another step back.

"Don't worry," Morgan whispered. "Skunks need to raise their tails to spray. They can't do that in tight spaces." Morgan stalled for a minute, holding her breath.

Sasha, accustomed to volunteers rattling about the pen while cleaning, eventually just closed her eyes and waited for Morgan to leave so she could go back to sleep.

"Whew, that was close." Lawren exhaled loudly when Morgan finally snapped the pen's lock shut.

"Nah." Morgan cavalierly quoted her mom. "Skunks are really reasonable, considering their potential."

The group headed back to the clinic so they could examine the crystal ornament.

"I don't see it," said Lucan. They looked at the star from every angle. It sparkled impressively in the sunlight, attesting to the nice cut of the glass. But as far as they could see, it was just glass. "What's so special about this thing?"

"I dunno." Anna was clearly as baffled as the rest of them.

"Whatever it is," said Morgan, "somebody wants it bad enough to break into the church *and* the wildlife center."

"*And* kidnap a kid." Lawren reminded them.

Morgan closed the box when she heard her mother drive up. She stuffed it into her backpack. "We'd better figure this out. And soon."

Mom pushed the door closed behind her with her foot as she carried a fawn into the clinic. "Morgan, I'm going to need help."

Morgan slid her pack under the desk and joined her mother in the treatment room. She held the fawn for her mother, wrapping one arm around its tiny body, holding its head by the muzzle with the opposite hand, and pulling it snuggly against her chest. It looked to be about four months old. Mom swabbed fresh puncture wounds that looked to Morgan like they had been delivered by a large dog. *Even in the city limits, a coyote would have finished the job.*

Lawren sucked her breath through her teeth, grimacing. "Ouch, that's gotta hurt." The holes penetrated the deer's head to the bone in several spots.

"It looks really spacey," said Morgan. The animal didn't struggle in her arms. Its eyes were glazed, and one ear drooped dramatically. It was in shock.

"It looks like the dog grabbed it by the head and shook it." Mom injected drugs Morgan knew were to reduce swelling and fight infection. They watched the veterinarian palpate the fawn's skull, spine and, finally each limb.

The animal wouldn't, or couldn't stand, but its tail wiggled, and it moved each of its four legs as it struggled weakly in Morgan's arms. "That's a good sign, right?" Morgan hoped.

"It doesn't feel like there's anything broken." Mom sounded somewhat more encouraged, "but I'll have to take X-rays to be sure."

"It looks really bad." Anna looked shaken.

Mom smiled at the girls, reassuring. "Show Anna how to fix a bottle of formula," she told Morgan.

Morgan recognized the redirect; Anna needed a distraction. The girl was very pale, and fainting wasn't pleasant. Mom gently picked up the fawn, and took it down the narrow hallway to the clinic's radiology room.

Morgan led her friends to the kitchen, where she mixed powdered lamb-milk-replacer formula with warm water, filled an empty plastic soda bottle, then stretched a rubber nipple over the opening.

It didn't take her mother long to finish taking her radiographs. She handed the fawn to Morgan and left to develop her film the old fashioned way, in dip tanks.

"Wanna feed it?" Morgan asked Anna.

Excitement edged out nerves. "Sure," she said. Morgan motioned Anna to the couch so she could place the fawn on the girl's lap.

Morgan showed her how to open and insert the nipple into the deer's mouth, then squeeze out a few drops of formula from the soft plastic bottle. Milk dribbled from the animal's mouth a few times before the fawn accepted the foreign object. Morgan circled the baby's face with her hand, covering the animal's eyes and massaging its face, encouraging it to swallow. It didn't take long for the fawn to instinctively push against Morgan's hand and swallow the warm formula. It finished the bottle in no time. Stomach full, it relaxed and started to look around the room, simultaneously swiveling its large ears and sniffing the air.

"It'll need some stitches, but I don't see anything broken." Mom looked happier when she returned. "Now I need to find someone to raise it."

"Don't look at me." Lucan waved hands both and shook his head an emphatic negative. "I'm swamped with raccoons."

Morgan snickered. She knew Lucan's kits were big enough now to eat on their own, but it would be another month before they'd be able to be housed at the sanctuary. Sure, he could sleep through the night now, but cleaning and feeding had become a royal pain. Raccoon kits are notoriously sloppy eaters, and they produce a mountain of poop, both of which they carelessly spread to every inch of their cage.

"Can I?" Anna surprised them all.

Mom was quiet as she considered it. "It would do best if it could be raised near wild deer and released as soon as possible," she said. "Deer habituate easily, and can become pests."

Morgan waited as her mom weighed the risks. Not a lot of the volunteers raised fawns. An adult deer that wasn't afraid of humans could be dangerous.

"We live by the forest." Anna seemed determined. "And there's a wild herd we feed."

Mom pursed her lips. "I need to talk to your parents first."

* * * * *

The end of the school year came and went like a whisper. It was as if the wind had turned a page in her life and Morgan barely noticed. She left middle school for the last time without a backward glance. Next year she would start high school, but today summer, with all its energy and activity, was calling.

The wildlife sanctuary was bustling with juvenile animals brought back by volunteer caregivers. As the animals matured over the next few months they would gradually be switched to their natural diets and released in the autumn, while food was still plentiful.

The summer solstice, Litha, at AWF was a hub of activity. The wildlife center's annual Nature Camp was in full swing. Morgan shaded her eyes. Kids invaded every corner of the sanctuary grounds. All day long volunteers had been giving tours of the Nature Trail and the animals that lived there.

Morgan, Lucan, and Lawren helped the last of the campers finish making birdhouses and decorating them with seeds and cobs of corn. What wasn't taken home by the kids would be stored and distributed to the animals during the winter solstice. Lucan attached the last colorful Indian corn cob to the traditional wreath, fanning the husk to the outside of the ring like a brilliant sunburst. Morgan recalled the vision quest she had shared with Lucan, and sighed. *Was it really six months ago?*

A fly buzzed around her head. "This really feels like the longest day of the year," she complained. She hadn't felt so hot and tired since . . . well . . . last summer.

"I forgot how hard this day is." Lawren forced a smile as she helped the last kid finish his project before steering him toward the parking lot and the waiting buses. "And how long."

"As if there isn't enough work to do in the summer," Morgan grumbled. The season was filled with cleaning, feeding, and watering. Nature Camp was the first of three annual wildlife center events. Still on the horizon were the volunteer appreciation picnic and the foundation's major fundraising event.

"Actually makes me miss the rain," said Lucan.

Morgan laughed. "I think you're finally becoming an Oregonian." Morgan had a new respect for the guy. After the May Day Masquerade fiasco she had been sure Lucan would quit volunteering for the wildlife center. His community service requirements had been completed long ago. And yet, here he was.

"You've gotta admit," said Lawren, "we got a lot done."

Morgan scanned the area. Tools and supplies littered the tables and floor. As usual, the campers hadn't put away anything. "There's a ton of clean-up still to do," she said. "And, now that everyone's gone, I want to take another look at that ornament. We're missing something."

Working together, it didn't take long to put everything into storage. She felt a cool breeze as clouds magically appeared in the sky. The shade gave Morgan a second wind. She collected the ornament box from Jerome's pen.

"Don't forget to empty the wishing well," Mom reminded her from across the yard.

Morgan waved, acknowledging she'd heard the request, before leading her friends to the wildlife center's wishing well. The natural stone ring was topped with a wooden roof from which hung a small bucket. Inside the rock cistern was a built-in metal lock box.

"I never noticed your wishing well is also a donation jar," said Lucan.

"Yup." Morgan opened the slotted door with a key. The strongbox was littered with torn paper notes. She gathered the messages along with the change from the bottom of the well. "As you can see," said Morgan, "we get a lot more wishes than donations." She left the door ajar. "We keep it open overnight to discourage vandals who think we hide our vast fortune here."

"What do you do with all the wishes?" Lucan asked.

"We burn them every month at the full moon," said Morgan, "to send them to heaven."

Lucan shook his head. "God seems to like rituals."

"Don't be silly," Morgan scoffed. "God doesn't need rituals. We do—to remind us to take the time to honor the Creator of all things."

Lucan raised his eyebrows at Lawren. His face was clear. *Your mother is a minister. Do you buy into all this?*

Lawren shrugged her shoulders. "I go to church every Sunday. Same diff."

"Go ahead," Morgan told them. "Make a wish." She took the ornament out of its box, looked toward the sky, and spoke her own wish out loud. "I wish I knew why someone wants this thing so badly."

"It's been quiet," said Lucan. "Maybe whoever wants it has given up by now."

"Maybe, but not likely," said Morgan. "They've gone through an awful lot of trouble for it so far."

"Aaaahhhh." Lawren screamed as large black wings beat down on her back. Cyrano, tether trailing behind, appeared from nowhere. His giant wings knocked Lawren's glasses off as the determined buzzard tried to push past her to get to Morgan . . . no, to get to the Christmas tree topper, which glittered in the sunlight like a giant jewel.

Lawren bumped into Morgan trying to escape the bird, nearly knocking her to the ground. Lucan caught her before she fell, but not before Morgan dropped the crystal star.

Cyrano landed between them, folded his wings, and looked up innocently before turning his attention back to his prize. He started to peck at the glass, greedily shoving it around on the ground.

Morgan righted herself. She could feel her face flush as she pushed away from Lucan. She scolded the errant vulture. "Not again, you little monster. How did you get away this time?" She looked around for the volunteer who should be watching him, but that person either hadn't missed the bird yet, or hadn't caught up with him.

Morgan stepped on Cyrano's leash to trap him, hoping her jeans and tennis shoes would protect her from the bird's strong beak. But Cyrano wasn't thinking about escape, concentrating instead on the bright red heart in the center of the ornament. *Probably attracted to the color*, thought Morgan. *Or the glitter.*

"He can't break anything, can he?" asked Lucan.

"I don't think so," said Morgan. "It's pretty solid."

"He sure loves sparkly things, doesn't he?" Lawren laughed, having recovered her glasses and her composure.

Morgan bent over to pick up the ornament before the vulture actually managed to break it. Before she could take it from him, the heart snapped open. A small leather pouch, folded over and tied with a thin leather strap, was stuffed inside.

"What's that?" Lawren took a step closer, forgetting about the vulture's mock attack.

"I'm not sure." Morgan pulled at the stiff ties. The pouch itself was soft and opened easily. She tipped the contents into her hand and gasped. Two rings slid out. One looked hand-carved. Dark and light woods polished to a smooth finish floated side-by-side changing positions once, like a Mobius. Morgan could see the details of each tree inside the wood. It felt alive. The second ring was also to-die-for—a gold band that twisted once, with a channel of small diamonds. An inscription etched in the metal read, *for eternity.* "They look like wedding bands," she said.

The rings tingled warmly in her hand. For one brief moment Morgan felt like she was sleep walking, out of step with time, as the rings told their story—one of lovers whose feelings began as soft and fragile as wood, then grew in into an enduring romance. Lucan's hand on Morgan's shoulder yanked her back to the here and now. She teetered, unsteady.

"You okay?" Blue eyes searched hers. "You disappeared on us for a minute."

Morgan nodded. Her attention was pulled to the ground as Cyrano bobbed up and down, begging for the return of his prize.

"Oh, thank goodness." Sonny was huffing by the time she caught up with the vulture. The volunteer pushed back a strand of hair that had escaped her waist-length gray braid. She tucked her tie-dyed tee-shirt back into her oversized overalls as best as her gloved hands would allow. "I thought he was gone for sure this time."

Morgan palmed the rings and hid them behind her back. She heaved a sigh, glad Sonny had come to collect the vulture before he stopped begging for his loot and started demanding it.

"Come here, you little hooligan." The elderly volunteer scooped up the eight-pound bird, snagging the tether before he could take off again. She nodded at the open star. "Oh. I hope he hasn't broken your decoration." She admonished the vulture before heading up the Nature Trail to Cyrano's mews. "You've been a naughty boy."

Lucan picked up the ornament and snapped it together. The internal hinge and joint closed seamlessly. "What a break. We might never have found that secret compartment."

"I bet this is what that crook is looking for." Morgan thanked God for granting her wish.

"No doubt." Lawren nodded her head vigorously. "Whatta you think they're worth?"

"A nice chunk of change," said Lucan. But he wasn't so sure. "Enough to have done what they did?"

Morgan's attention floated between the well's lock box and the ornament locket. *To discourage vandals who think we hide our vast fortune here.* And then it hit her. "Maybe they don't know what's inside the star? Maybe they think it's more, or a clue to more."

"That's it," Lawren exclaimed. Then she had second thoughts. "They know about the star and its "treasure" because of the diary. But how did they get the journal?"

"Don't know," Morgan admitted. "When we figure that out, we might figure out *who*."

"Either way, we need to get the rings back to Anna's family," said Lucan. "And take the topper back to the church."

"Eventually," said Morgan.

"What do you mean . . . eventually?" asked Lawren.

"Don't you see?" said Morgan. "Now that we know *what* they're after, we can set a trap, and catch them red-handed."

"Are you crazy?" Lucan was aghast. "At the very least, we need to turn these over to the cops."

Morgan shook her head. "If we do that, the crook will just disappear, and we'll never figure it out. We need to catch them."

"You watch too much crime TV," said Lawren. "Let's just give the stuff back and be done with this caper."

But Morgan was adamant. "If we do that we might be putting a target on Anna and her family. I know you don't want to do that." She looked at Lucan expectantly.

Lawren grinned, fully committed to the coercion.

"The crook broke into both the church and the wildlife center to get this thing," Morgan reminded him. "There's no telling what they'd do to Anna's family if they were desperate."

"Or confronted." Lucan seemed determined to put the kibosh on the adventure. "Leave crime fighting to the police."

Morgan ignored him. She could feel her excitement grow as an idea formulated in her mind. "What about our auction?" The wildlife center sold much of the goods donated throughout the year at their annual fund raising event in August. "We can take a picture of the ornament box in front of all the stuff we collect for the sale and post it in the newspaper."

Lawren allowed herself to get caught up in the scheme. "I get it. Only the crook will know the star is in the box."

Morgan shook her head vigorously, "When they try to steal it, we'll expose them."

"You and what army?" Lucan crossed his arms, but Morgan could see his resolve wavering.

She grinned like the cat that finally cornered the canary. "I've got a plan."

* * * * *

"Achoo." Morgan sneezed into her elbow. She surveyed Anna's dusty family attic. Wooden beams reached from floor to ceiling in the large, half-finished room lit only by a single suspended bulb. The belongings of several generations filled the space. Morgan, Anna, and Mrs. Wildling were collecting things to sell at the wildlife center's annual fundraiser and auction.

"I've never seen so much stuff." Morgan pried opened the first of three wooden crates stacked on top of each other. Inside was a stash of old comic books. "Whoa." She pulled out a few of the magazines and waved them at Anna. "Someone's sure to want these. I wonder how much they're worth."

"Those belonged to my cousins," said Mrs. Wildling. "I don't think they're collectors' pieces. Leo and Uri just liked to read comics, and my aunt was happy they'd read anything at all." She chuckled. "They weren't particularly good students."

"Gross." Anna grimaced and wiped her grimy hands on her jeans. "I can't remember the last time I was in here."

"I can," said her mother. "It was just after Grandmamma died. We were in here with your Uncle Joe going through some of her things."

"Oh yeah," Anna bristled. "I didn't want you to give her stuff away. I still don't."

Morgan paused, feeling a bit like an unwelcome scavenger.

Mrs. Wildling's stern expression told her daughter she wouldn't tolerate another argument. "We agreed it's been long enough." Her voice was resolute. "And it's for a good cause."

"I know." Anna relented, turning to Morgan. "I really *do* want to help the animals."

A spider crawled across Morgan's arm. She jumped back and brush-slapped both of her arms furiously. "Yuuuuk," she shuddered. "I hate bugs."

Anna giggled.

"We'll haul what we can today by truck," Mrs. Wildling continued. "I'll have any heavier items delivered." She pulled aside boxes and bags for Morgan and Anna to carry downstairs.

They spent the next hour sorting through things. It seemed they'd hardly made a dent in the stuff. Suitcases and trunks were full of clothing. Blankets and comforters spilled from shelves. Morgan fingered beautiful hand-made quilts and embroidered bedding. There were at least two baby cribs full of old toys, along with strollers and other baby junk. *Grandma must have been a hoarder. She didn't get rid of anything.*

Morgan shivered looking around at all the dark spaces. *I wonder what else is living in this attic?* She half-expected to see a rat or worse, roaches, but the group appeared to be alone.

Or were they?

Movement caught the corner of Morgan's eye. She turned to see the specter of a man not much taller than she standing in front of a roll-top desk. She blinked twice, trying to check her imagination, but the apparition didn't disappear. Her jaw dropped. She looked to Anna and Mrs. Wildling, wanting to warn them, but they seemed oblivious of the shadowy invader. Morgan turned back to the phantom. She squinted, trying to see him better. *What's he doing?* The ghost looked to be rifling through some papers inside the desk. Curiosity squelched Morgan's fear. *What's he looking for?* She took a step closer, but just as suddenly as he had appeared, he was gone.

"Did you see that?" Morgan stammered.

"What dear?" Mrs. Wildling and Anna stopped their rummaging to look at the fishing gear near Morgan's feet. "You can take that if you think it will sell."

Morgan stepped over the tackle and snaked her way to the roll-top desk. It sat lonely and abandoned in a corner of the room. She examined the old piece of furniture. The lock was badly scratched, but the front casing was closed. Morgan furrowed her brow. *I could've sworn it was open.* She tugged at the stiff lift rail. Dry tambour slats scraped along the wooden tracks. *Yuk.* Morgan scowled. *More dust.* An assortment of ledgers and loose papers protruded from vertical organizer shelves inside the desk. Morgan shuffled through them, but didn't come across anything particularly interesting.

"My great-grandfather made that," said Mrs. Wildling. "Someone might buy it as a computer table."

"Maybe." But Morgan was preoccupied. Something just didn't seem right. She studied the worn writing table, turning her head sideways to look it from an angle that took better advantage of the available light. And then she noticed it. The dust on the tabletop was uneven. *It looks like something has been taken. Is this where the crook got the journal? How? And when?* In the years since Anna's grandmother had died practically anyone could have come up here and stolen the journal, invited or not. How many people wondered if the family had truly lost their wealth? Or believe that someone had secretly hidden it, and it was waiting for some determined treasure hunter to find it?

Morgan pursed her lips and looked up slowly. She slid the roll-top closed without a word. *I don't want to scare Anna or Mrs. Wildling,* she thought, *but whatever's going on didn't start at the church. It started in this attic.* She looked over at them. *Should I warn them that someone broke into their house?* She decided against it, considering the flimsy evidence.

The trio spent the rest of the morning boxing and bagging kitchenware, books, knickknacks, and clothing. Then they carried them down the stairs and out to the front lawn where volunteers loaded them onto a beat-up old pick-up truck to drive it to the wildlife center.

"I was hoping there'd be more for the silent auction table where we could get better money," said Mrs. Wildling. "Much of this will have to be sold as yard-sale items." She sounded disappointed as she served the girls lemonade while they waited for the truck to return. "What fortune *great*-grandfather made in the lumber business," she explained, "grandfather lost in the depression, I'm afraid."

"Is that what happened to the money?" Anna asked.

Morgan listened closely, feeling a little guilty for keeping the rings they'd found inside the tree topper a secret. *It's for their own safety,* she justified.

Mrs. Wildling nodded and smiled, shaking her head. "He was a bit of a schemer, your grandpapa," she said. "Always looking for the easy way." She sighed. "I think my brother inherited that from him."

Mrs. Wildling smiled sadly. "It's all gone, my little Anoushka."

"How come I don't remember Uncle Joe?"

"I'm not surprised. He's been gone a long time." Mrs. Wildling fidgeted as though it was not a subject she wanted to discuss. She relented with a loud sigh. "He got drunk one night with his friends and they got arrested trying to rob a convenience store. He didn't know it," she said, "but one of them had a gun."

Anna caught her breath. "Did they shoot someone?"

"No, thank God," Mrs. Wildling crossed herself, "but they caused a lot of damage." She passed the girls a plate of cookies. "He's going to be in prison for a long time."

Morgan took a bite out of her cookie, taking in the private drama. The Wildlings seemed to be a family of success and scandal, of love and loss.

"Why didn't you tell me?" asked Anna. "Did you ever see him again?"

Mrs. Wildling shook her head. "The last time I saw my little brother was that day in the attic. He was arrested that night." She patted cookie crumbs off her long dress. "You were very young, and these are not things I want you to concern yourself with."

Bang. The girls both jumped, then laughed at each other when they realized the noise had been the back-fire of the old truck come to collect another load. It sputtered loudly as the vehicle rattled up to the curb and parked in front of the house. Mrs. Wildling clapped her hands. "Back to work."

* * * * *

Lucan listed to one side as he carried the crate into the raccoon enclosure. It was a lot heavier now than when he'd taken it home just a few months ago. The four raccoon kits he'd fostered were weaned and ready to be left at the wildlife center to be transitioned for release back into the wild.

Morgan filled the large community food bowl with dry puppy chow, fruits, and vegetables, as Lucan set the crate down carefully and opened the door. "What now?" He asked, warily eyeing the five raccoons that already occupied the pen.

"Now we get outta here and give them some space," said Morgan. "This could take a while."

They heard growling and huffing as they headed back to the clinic. Morgan took Lucan's elbow to keep him from turning back, then slid her hand down to take his. She could feel his heart tug. Letting go is the toughest part of the job. "They always sound like they want to kill each other at first," she reassured him. "You just wait; within a couple of hours they'll be best buds."

"I guess we should get back," said Lucan. The wildlife center's annual 4th of July Volunteer Appreciation BBQ was underway on the front lawn.

"We've got a lot of great stuff collected for the yard sale this year." Lawren trotted over to Morgan and Lucan with a big grin. She brushed a stray hair from her mouth as her eyes dropped for a second to their clasped hands.

Morgan flushed and let go of Lucan.

"I'll get us some food," said Lucan.

It was a perfect summer day. Volunteers and their families were laughing, playing badminton and horseshoes on the lawn. The smell of hot dogs, hamburgers, and fresh buttered corn wafted from the BBQ, where Uncle Rick was grilling. Groups loitered, swapping their favorite animal stories. Outside the wildlife center, Morgan knew most of these people didn't socialize with each other. Here, no matter how different they were, they were drawn together by their love of animals. Morgan thought on all that happened at the sanctuary on a daily basis, and felt blessed.

She joined her friends by the wishing well. As they ate, they laughed and talked—about graduating from middle school, starting high school, and plans for college. Morgan's eyes roamed from one person to another—some she'd just come to know, others she'd grown up with. *They say every encounter and each relationship has a different purpose*, she thought. Her eyes stopped at Lucan, and her stomach fluttered.

Summer isn't about gaining or losing, Mom had told her, it's about tending to what you have. And there is always plenty of work to be done—watering and weeding, cleaning and caring for young animals; waiting until they are old enough and big enough to be released into the wild.

It's nice to have a day just for play. Morgan lay down on the grass, clasping her hands behind her head, enjoying the sunshine.

"We need to take a picture for the newspaper article." Anna woke Morgan with a start. She blinked and rubbed dry eyes. The crowd had thinned considerably. *How long was I asleep*, she wondered? "Mama's collected all the stuff for the yard sale in one of the barn stalls," Anna persisted, "and I made sure the Christmas ornament box was front and center." She was anxious to find out who had stolen her great-grandmother's journal, and why they wanted the tree topper. Morgan felt a twinge of guilt about not telling Anna or her family about the rings they'd found. *Just until this escapade is over*, she told herself, *and the Wildlings are safe*.

Lucan gave Morgan a hand-up. The two of them went to the clinic to get the camera, then met Lawren and Anna in the barn.

Morgan blinked as her eyes adjusted from the bright sunshine to the shade of the barn. Her skin prickled as they walked past animal enclosures towards the last stall before the center aisle. It was cool in the large, metal building. "Wow, this is as much as we've ever collected," she said. The door to the 12X12 cubicle was barely closeable, full to near-overflow. "We should make a tidy sum this year."

Anna beamed, apparently having resolved her issues with losing her grandmother's precious things. "Mama loves yard sales."

Morgan took several shots before she was satisfied with the picture. Dead center, you couldn't miss the wooden ornament box. "Aunt Jackie will send this to the newspaper with a press release the week before our event." She smiled, satisfied. "Whoever wants this decoration won't be able to miss it."

"The trap is set." Lawren clapped and rubbed her hands together dramatically.

"Are you sure you don't want to get the cops involved?" Lucan still had his doubts.

"We can't be sure it'll work," Morgan reasoned. "Besides, Uncle Rick will be there, and he's security enough."

"Why do you have the event August 1st," Lucan asked. "It could be pretty hot."

"It might," Morgan agreed. In Oregon the summer is almost as unpredictable as the winter; one day could be over 100°, the next it could be a comfortable 80°. It might even rain. She shrugged her shoulders. "First Harvest is as good a time as any. After that we're busy getting animals ready for release before the wild berries all burn out."

* * * * *

"The ones that want to climb up your pant legs are probably yours," Morgan told Lucan as she scraped piles of raccoon poop from the corner of the enclosure into her scooper and dumped it into a garbage bag. "Don't let them," she insisted. "It's time they grew up."

Lucan squirted the two young raccoons nearest his feet with the hose before redirecting the stream to fill their large bathtub with clean water. The animals pinned their ears and hightailed it back under the large claw-foot tub, screaming their objections. Impatient, the raccoons chirred and hissed at each other. Each wanted to be the first to wade into the cold water or to pick out its favorite treats from the food bowls.

A fly buzzed too close to Morgan's head. It was only eight o'clock in the morning and already it was hot enough for the insects to be out doing their worst. "I hate bugs," Morgan grumbled as she swatted at it.

"At least this pen doesn't have many wasps." Lucan ducked and sent a shower of water into the air, chasing the pesky bugs away from himself and the animal foods. "We could be cleaning one of the raptor pens," he said. In the summer the raw meat fed to the birds-of-prey attracted hungry yellow jackets.

"Don't worry, they're more interested in the food than in us." Morgan exhaled a frustrated breath, hoping Lucan wouldn't just drop what he was doing and run from the pen. He wouldn't be the first. "You just have to be careful," she said.

Admirably, Lucan stood his ground.

Summer was beginning its final month. It was the busy season at the wildlife center and the workload was at its peak. Most of the enclosures were full of animals; cleaning had become a long and tedious job. The waist-high pasture grass lay on the ground waiting to be baled for hay. Volunteers had spent the past week with a weed whacker, trimming and edging to spruce up the place for today's event.

Morgan's eyes were pulled to the activity behind the veterinary clinic where the sanctuary's annual fund raising event, *Wildlife Rhythms*, was being set up. The large open area was not used during the dark half of the year because it collected standing water. Tables and chairs were gathered around a make-shift stage, where a volunteer band was setting up and checking sound levels. Morgan winced at yet another screech from the P.A. system. Anna and her mother were decorating the auction and sales tables. Food and drink vendors would be arriving soon.

"It's a good thing you have so much property," said Lucan, "to keep all the racket away from the animals."

"I'm glad it's only once a year," Morgan sniffed. She reached into her bucket and pulled out a bag of squishy orange pellets, and grinned at Lucan. "Ready for a treat?"

Lucan looked at the occupants of the pen, who were suddenly unnaturally quiet. "Me?" he asked, "or the raccoons?"

"Both." Morgan dropped the pungent pellets into the water of the bathtub; they floated and spread out silently along the bottom. Black noses quivered at the intoxicating new aroma. The food bowls, the trees, and the platforms were abandoned as the raccoons converged on ramp that led up into the tub. Soon every animal was splashing in the pool, fishing for the small orange prizes. "Fish eggs." Morgan wrinkled her nose at Lucan. "A raccoon delicacy."

Finished with their chores, Morgan and Lucan watched the animals play. The plan she had hatched was obviously on both their minds.

"I can't talk you out of your crazy scheme, can I?" Lucan asked, as if he didn't already know what her answer would be. Still, he offered, "it's not too late to call the cops."

"It'll be fine." Morgan took a deep breath and picked up her stuff, ready to face the event, *and* whoever wanted the Christmas tree topper and its hidden treasure.

Anna, Lawren, Lucan, and Morgan took turns keeping eyes on the auction and sales tables, in case someone expressed an interest in any Christmas ornaments, and watching the barn stall featured in the newspaper article, where the crook would think the tree topper was locked. But the afternoon wore into evening without a single suspicious thing.

"Looks like this scheme is going to be a bust," said Lawren. She and Morgan were taking their turn waiting in the cool barn. She looked as tired and discouraged as Morgan felt. "What's Plan B?" she asked.

"I got nothing," Morgan admitted, frustrated. "I was so sure this would work." She wracked her brain for what could have gone wrong. *Maybe the person didn't see the newspaper article?*

"Maybe Lucan was right," Lawren shrugged her thin shoulders, "and the guy gave up when the school year ended."

Morgan winced before reluctantly admitting Lucan might have called it correctly. "Maybe." *But why would the school year make any difference?* She felt her cell phone vibrate. It was probably Lucan calling it quits. This caper was obviously a failure. The event was almost over and most of the guests had already gone. The band had finished nearly an hour ago. The vendors had locked up their trailers for the night; they'd come back for them in the morning.

"We just had a woman ask about decorations." Lucan's voice was tense. "I told her we don't have any."

Morgan's heart raced as she stuffed her phone back into her pocket and turned to her best friend, holding her pointer finger in front of her lips. *The game is afoot*, as the famous detective Sherlock Homes would have said. If this person was their suspect, they would know soon.

But fifteen minutes later they were still waiting. Morgan sighed in defeat, and phoned Lucan to call off the alert. Apparently the person had been an early Christmas shopper after all, and their would-be thief had given them the slip.

The call of the wildlife center's screech owl, Click, pierced the quiet of the night and echoed eerily off the metal walls of the dark barn. It was a sound Morgan hadn't heard in a long time as the owl was quite old, and she wasn't often at the sanctuary at night. She furrowed her brow and strained to hear. *Is that shuffling coming toward us?* Morgan pulled Lawren into the neighboring stall and they hid in the shadows.

Something, or someone, startled the red-tailed hawk being housed in the stall down and across the aisle from Click. Morgan cringed when she heard the bird crash into the wall of its pen, praying the animal hadn't re-broken its wing. She heard the shuffling again. *There is someone coming.* Morgan thought. *And he's heading this way.*

"Damned birds," a low voice growled.

Lawren grabbed Morgan's arm, eyes wide with terror. They watched the shadowy figure of a man not much taller than Morgan fumble with the lock on the barn stall before snapping it with a very large bolt cutter. The specter disappeared inside. The girls heard the click of a flashlight.

Crash. Bang. Scrape. The man was not careful as he searched through the stuff in the stall, ostensibly looking for the ornament box. "Dammit. Where is it?" he hissed.

Morgan texted Lucan, fairly certain the intruder couldn't see the glow of her cell phone: 9-1-1. She bit her lower lip. She'd forgotten to turn off her phone's touch-tone, a feature she left on to avoid accidentally butt-dialing anyone. "Beep, beep, beep." The metal barn was like an echo chamber. She quickly hit send.

"Who's there?" the man barked.

The girls held their breaths, hoping the guy would believe he imagined the sound.

He didn't. His flashlight emerged from the stall and streamed down the barn aisle. It wouldn't be long before he'd come into the stall the girls were hiding in, and they'd be trapped. "Get outta there," he ordered.

Unable to think of another option, Morgan and Lawren did as they were told. Lawren stayed close behind Morgan, who was using her hand to block the blinding light shining directly into their eyes. All they could see was the shadow of a stocky man holding a flashlight in one hand and a large bolt cutter in the other. But there it was again, that overwhelming smell of stale cigarettes. The specter in the Wildling attic flashed in her mind, making her dizzy for a moment.

"What do you want?" Morgan demanded, hoping she sounded braver than she felt.

"You know exactly what I'm after," he growled. "Now hand it over."

"Yo...you'd better get outta here right now," Lawren stammered. "We called the cops."

"Then you'd better give me what I want quickly," he said. He didn't look in any particular hurry.

The overhead lights flipped on, revealing a face Morgan had seen before. *Derek Angst.*

"Hey, you're the Easter Bunny." Lawren seemed to have forgotten her fear for a moment.

"Leave them alone," Lucan demanded, as he ran toward them from the barn entrance. It was he who had flipped on the light switch.

Derek didn't look intimidated as he faced the teenage boy.

Just then, taking advantage of the distraction, Rick stepped from around the corner of the center aisle and grabbed the stocky man from behind, sending both the flashlight and the bolt cutter to the ground. Morgan's uncle spun the intruder around and clocked him in the face, dropping the man with one well-placed punch.

Thank goodness. Morgan breathed a sigh of relief. Lucan had not come alone.

Derek was *not* a fighter. He did not get up again. The grubby and disheveled man lay cringing on the dirt floor.

"*Joseph!*" Mrs. Wildling's cry interrupted the scuffle. In all the excitement Morgan hadn't seen her or Anna run into the barn, followed closely by Mom and Aunt Jackie.

"You know this guy?" Rick sounded incredulous.

Pale faced, Mrs. Wildling nodded. "Anna, meet your Uncle Joe."

Autumn Reaping

"This is the piece we were missing." Anna dropped a stack of hand-written letters on the wildlife center desk in front of Lucan, Lawren, and Morgan. "Letters from my grandmother to Mama and Uncle Joe."

"Is that what was taken from the roll-top desk?" Morgan scanned the documents.

Her friends gaped at her. "How did you know that?" asked Anna.

Morgan told them about the ghostly image she had seen in the attic, and the disturbed dust on the roll-top desk. "Of course I thought it was the journal," she admitted.

"It was," said Anna. "They were inside."

"So that's where Uncle Joe first found the diary," said Lucan.

"Yeah," Lawren nodded. "And stole it."

"He swears he didn't steal it," Anna insisted. Clearly, she wanted to believe her Uncle.

"I can't believe they didn't call the cops." Lucan shook his head. It had been a week since *Wildlife Rhythms* and Morgan and her friends had been annoyingly left out of the adult cover-up of their recent criminal discoveries. "They certainly wanted to punish me. What made him think I had the journal?" he asked.

"He didn't," said Morgan, "at first. He saw the topper in the article in the newspaper about the Holiday Bazaar."

"That's why he broke into the church," said Lawren. "He knew it had been donated."

"Yup." Morgan nodded. "When he didn't find it he tore the place apart. He must've found your mom's counseling file on Lucan."

"So he knew I was doing community service at the wildlife center for stealing the ornament."

"And when we took the journal from the trailer, he knew we were onto him," said Morgan.

"But we missed the letters stashed with my great-grandmother's diary in the desk." Anna got back to her story.

"You mean before your uncle stole it," said Lawren.

Anna's face tightened. "My uncle confessed to taking the journal the day he and his friends were arrested," she admitted. "It was in his pocket when they hauled him in. It's been in a locker in the sheriff's property room all this time."

"Until he *escaped*." Lawren jumped ahead of the story.

Morgan had noticed that Lawren was acting a lot braver since their nighttime encounter in the barn, and maybe just a bit more dramatic.

"*Actually*, he was released on good behavior," said Anna. "He says he didn't read the diary until then."

"Which means he couldn't have known about the treasure hidden in the ornament," Morgan concluded.

"Unless he believed the rumors floating around town of hidden family money," Lawren insisted.

"We can't know if he'd even heard the stories." *If they'd learned anything in the past year,* Morgan thought, *it's how fast things can snowball.* No one had intended their actions to turn into a criminal adventure. "He must've stashed the letters someplace else in the RV."

Anna nodded. "That's why we didn't find them."

Lawren shrugged and pushed her glasses back over the bridge of her nose.

Morgan read out loud from one of the letters. "This letter is dated from the 1930s, and it mentions the Christmas tree topper. *I love your father dearly, my darlings, but he really has no head for business. We have lost so much in this Depression. I didn't want to lose everything.*" It went on to explain how she had hidden *her most valuable treasures* in the ornament to prevent her husband from selling them in a desperate attempt to resolve some of their losses."

Lawren clung to her indignation as she brought them back to recent happenings. "When he didn't find the topper at the wildlife center he decided he needed to go to the source."

"But he kidnapped Zane instead of me." Lucan shook his head. "So why didn't he go to jail? Kidnapping is serious."

"Because the kidnapping was reported as a prank." Lawren put her hands on her hips.

"I'm sorry I got you all involved." Anna explained. "I put the ornament in your bag by accident." She turned to Lawren. "And Uncle Joe never meant to hurt anyone. He let Zane go right away."

Morgan shuddered, wondering where they might be if Joe had actually captured Lucan. She skimmed the rest of letter and turned to Lawren. "It never actually says what's hidden in the ornament."

Anna shrugged her shoulders. "We don't know."

Morgan pursed her lips. "We do," she admitted. "Wait here." She left the clinic and headed to the Nature Trail and Jerome's pen to retrieve the ornament one last time.

When she got back she showed Anna the secret compartment in the heart of the tree topper. She handed the leather pouch to Anna and the Christmas decoration to

Lawren. "It's time these were returned to their rightful owners."

Anna gasped when she opened the bag and emptied the beautiful wedding bands into her hand. Morgan was glad when the girl didn't ask how long they'd known about the rings.

"You know, your uncle really sucks at being a crook," said Lucan. "But maybe he doesn't deserve to go to prison."

"Mama begged them not to report him to the police," said Anna. "She was afraid he'd be locked up for a really long time because this would be his second offense."

"What happens now?" asked Lawren.

"I heard them talking . . ." said Anna. "Uncle Joe has to make rep . . . repr . . ."

"Reparations?" Morgan finished.

"Yeah. Uncle Joe's going to stay with us until he can get his feet underneath him." Anna took a deep breath. "And, he has to work for the church and the wildlife center to pay for any damages."

"And quit smoking," Lawren quipped.

Great, Morgan thought, *another crook at the wildlife center performing community service.* Then she thought back on the past year with a wistful smile. *Of course, I guess that's how all this all began.*

* * * * *

Eight sets of brown eyes obscured by black masks watched Lucan, Morgan, and her mom from the rafters of the pen. Morgan steeled herself for the unpleasant task ahead. It was the end of another summer and time to release the juvenile raccoons, while their natural foods, primarily berries and overpopulated small prey animals, were plentiful. Hormones and instinct would finish the job of making them wild again.

"Let's do it." Mom slipped on heavy leather welding gloves and goggles and prepared to do battle. She wore full protective gear. "These animals won't come out of the pen nearly as easily as they went in."

Morgan and Lucan followed her into the pen; she carried a broom while he lugged in a large crate, balancing it on the top of his forward foot. They also wore goggles and gloves.

Lucan scanned the cage. "I can't tell mine from the others," he said without a smile. "And they don't seem to remember me."

"They don't need a mom anymore." Morgan nodded at the other raccoons in the pen. "You've been replaced."

One by one they corralled, then grabbed and crated each of the juvenile raccoons. And it got tougher as each animal figured out what was in store for it in turn. The scent of expressed anal glands, feces, and urine wafted through the air when they were done.

"Phew." Lucan grimaced, waving a hand across his face. Morgan wrinkled her nose. *That* was a smell she'd never get used to. She and Lucan carried the heavy crates of raccoons out of the pens and loaded them into Rick's truck.

Bang. The cage bars rattled as the largest raccoon threw itself at the door.

Lucan startled. They watched the raccoon try to chew its way out of air vents too small to push its muzzle through. The animal defecated out of sheer exhaustion. Morgan giggled as Lucan held his nose and tried to recover his dignity.

"Ugh," Rick pulled a face, "just what I want to put in my truck."

"We always wash and de-flea it when we're done," Jackie assured him. It didn't stop her husband from grumbling.

Everyone removed their soiled gear and handed them to Morgan's mom. "Whew." She held the leathers away from her clothing and pulled a face. "Good thing you won't need these at the release site. They're going directly into the washing machine."

Rick drove to the release site with the truck windows wide open. The terrified raccoons were eerily quiet. Lucan's face was strained. Morgan felt sorry for him and wanted to hold his hand, but didn't dare to in front of her aunt and uncle. She knew this release was as scary for Lucan as it was for the kits he'd raised. The animals would have to adapt, and quickly, if they were going to survive in the wild.

"That crate has been open for nearly twenty minutes," Lucan whispered as the four of them sat on the tailgate of the truck waiting for the raccoons to finally leave their containers. The animals' open enclosures faced the edge of freedom, but the creatures inside were afraid to move.

"That's the way it happens sometimes." Jackie swatted at an insect that buzzed too close to her face. "You fight to get them into the crate. Then you fight to kick them out."

Finally, two of them stepped cautiously from the protection of their crates. Once outside, they raced blindly up the nearest trees. Not until they were twenty feet off the ground did they realize they'd each chosen a different tree. They called to each other piteously, scanning the area wide-eyed, each hoping the other would find a way to cross the divide.

Morgan couldn't help herself. She took Lucan's hand as he looked sadly after them.

The next four raccoons stepped out of the crates, curiosity conquering their fear. The animals ambled down to the river, exploring along the way. They chirred to each other comfortingly.

"They know what they're looking for, right?" asked Lucan.

"They've had it all," said Morgan. "Small fish, eggs, insects, even leaves and fruits." But today they only nibbled at nature's bounty. They weren't hungry. In fact, they'd never been hungry a day in their lives. The raccoons explored the shadowy slope down to the familiarity of the water and the surprises that lived along the river's edge.

The last two raccoons huddled together in the back of their crate, apparently hoping to go unnoticed, maybe even to be returned to the wildlife center.

"Not quite ready for freedom, I guess," said Lucan.

"I can't blame them," said Morgan. "Independence is scary when you're so young. Raccoon kits usually stay with their moms until she has the next litter the following spring." Morgan tapped the back of the crate, hoping to scare them out.

"Come on guys," Rick said to the stragglers. "We can't wait forever."

Morgan tilted the container, encouraging them to come out. But raccoon fingers clung to the window slats, hanging on for dear life. "We can't keep you," Morgan insisted. "Winter's on its way and the pickings only get slimmer."

Lucan helped Morgan tilt the crate higher. Eventually, the kids had to shake the raccoons from the safety of their enclosure. "Come on guys, there is no dignity in this." Morgan huffed with the effort. "You might as well just come out!"

Unable to hang on any longer, the two raccoons finally rolled out of the kennel. Shocked, they scrambled to their feet and dashed into the brush, kicking up dirt and gravel in their wake.

While Rick and Lucan loaded the empty crates into the back of the truck, Morgan watched the raccoons disappear into the forest. Lucan tore open a large bag of dog food they'd brought with them, and piled it onto the ground—a little something to give them a few days to acclimate to their second chance.

* * * * *

"I've wanted to see that movie for a long time." Morgan tried to act natural as she sat in the hard plastic chair Lucan had pulled out for her. They were in the food court at Towne Center Mall, just outside the Twenty-Plex movie theatre. "Pixar always has such great music," she said. *That sounds so lame,* but she was way too nervous to be casual. The theme song of the animated movie played in her head as she tried to relax. It was a just a few days before she and her friends would start their first year in high school. It was her fourteenth birthday. And, it was her first *real* date. She pretended not to notice her aunt and mother sitting just a few tables over, chatting and having coffee. *I can't wait 'til I can drive.*

If Lucan was uncomfortable about the chaperones, he didn't show it as he sat down and slid the plate of burger and fries toward her. "Lawren told me you were learning to play *Let It Go* on the piano for your recital." He took a long sip of his soda.

"I have to play a classical piece." Morgan took a small bite of French fry for something to do, but so she wouldn't be talking with a full mouth. She shrugged. "But I get to choose a number for fun too."

They discussed the movie while they ate, laughing at their favorite punch lines. When the last bite was finished and they seemed to have run out of jokes, Lucan reached into the back pocket of his jeans and pulled out a soft-wrapped package. "Happy birthday," he said handing it her.

Her heart thumped wildly. She looked around the room to see if anyone in the crowded building had noticed a moment that would probably be etched in her memory for the rest of her life. *Nope.*

She carefully peeled open the gift paper and tipped a black and white braided leather bracelet into her hand, and gasped. "It's beautiful. I love it." The soft ties looped to a silver infinity symbol.

Lucan took it from her and fastened it around her wrist. "To remind you of our adventure."

Morgan fingered the band and reflected on the last year. "Black and white like the raccoons," she said. "*And* the mixed-up costumes." She smiled as she toyed with the amulet. "An infinity symbol like the rings we found."

Lucan shrugged. "I was hoping it would keep you out of trouble." He rubbed the back of his neck. "I looked it up on the internet. Black is supposed to help keep away anything bad, while white attracts the good."

And the infinity symbol? Morgan's brow furrowed.

Mom rescued them before the growing silence got totally awkward. "Time to get going," she said.

Morgan's thoughts were a jumble on the drive home; about Lucan, about the stag with the comet-like scar. Although she was excited about her freshman year in high school, she was reluctant to let the last season of her childhood go. September predicted an Indian summer, bright and warm well into autumn. The glint of sunlight flashing on the car window as the trees rushed by on the drive home was like a daytime storm. She could feel change looming on the horizon and, for once, she was reluctant to have anything change. Morgan liked things the way they were.

Giving Thanks

"Can you believe Thano dumped me?" Lawren was outraged. "He didn't want to be *tied down*." She stressed her last two words with dramatic air quotes.

Morgan looked over her best friend's shoulder to the football teams' lunch table where Thano was laughing and joking with the high school jocks. She blinked twice. *He doesn't even look like the same guy.* The scrawny boy from Middle School was gone. Thano looked like he had grown three inches over the summer, and had gained at least ten pounds of muscle at football camp. *He actually looks kinda cute*, she thought. "What happened to his glasses?"

"Contact lenses," Lawren sniffed. "He's even dropped out of band so he could play in the games. Bet he's not worried about being *tied down* to a cheerleader." More air quotes.

"Doesn't really matter any way," Morgan said as she tugged her cardigan closed over her own developing bust line. "The school discourages freshman from dating."

"Like *that's* gonna happen." Lawren pushed her glasses over the bridge of her nose. While most of the kids had grown during the summer, Lawren looked like she was going to be a late bloomer. She was still tiny. And flat.

Morgan grabbed her schedule from her backpack. The usual freshman classes — algebra, band, honors English, biology . . . and health ed. *That's another name for sex education.* Morgan puffed out a noisy sigh. *Like we don't already know what's what.* Morgan had wanted to take music *and* art, but could choose only one. And, she'd prefer cooking over sex education any day of the week, but only seniors were allowed to take the popular culinary course.

The girls compared schedules across the table. "Looks like we've got band, PE, and health together," said Lawren. Her schedule didn't include any AP classes.

"And homeroom," Morgan reminded her as she fiddled with the infinity charm on her leather bracelet. She hadn't seen her boyfriend all day. *It still sounds so weird to say that.* She felt herself flush, and was glad no one could read her thoughts. Most of the kids in homeroom were the same ones they'd gone through middle school with.

"Speaking of homeroom, where's Lucan?" Lawren asked as she opened a bag of chips and started to munch. "I didn't see him this morning."

Morgan shrugged, pretending not to care — about Lucan or the chips. Her mouth watered. Chips were something she had had to curtail or suffer the acne breakout that inevitably followed, courtesy of her new hormones. She took a bite of her apple.

The girls ate quietly, watching the hierarchy around them reveal itself. Freshmen were clearly not even on the radar yet. The noise level of the room grew as friends found each other and caught up on the latest gossip — who had broken up, who had hooked up. Teams they were going "to cream." Plans were made for "the best year ever."

"You're dating a sophomore." Lucan startled Morgan when he materialized behind her and plunked his tray full of food down next to hers.

Morgan raised her brows as she inventoried his tray. *Guys sure eat a lot.*

Lucan was too excited to even wait for her response. "I managed to test back to my grade level," he grinned, "thanks to all the tutoring.

Morgan caught herself staring at his ice-blue eyes and black curls. He looked the same, but things had definitely changed since their date. *He's as handsome as any guy here,* she thought. *I can't believe he's dating me.* Morgan tried to be nonchalant. "I knew you could do it," she said. In truth, it hadn't even occurred to her that he'd still want to test up. She'd been looking forward to taking classes together.

"Congrats." Lawren grinned. "That explains why we haven't seen you today." She fanned her face and exhaled dramatically, as if she, a lowly freshman, was in the presence of total hotness. She got over it quickly enough. "Sophomores have a different schedule," she said, as she collected her stuff. "See ya. I know you two lovebirds want to be alone."

Morgan blushed, but Lucan acted as if he hadn't heard the remark. He dove into his food.

"It's time to release Anna's deer," said Morgan, finishing her food more gingerly. "Wanna come with us this weekend?"

"Sure," he said. "Sounds like fun." Then a shadow crossed his face. "Is Uncle Joe going to be there? I think I've seen enough of him for one lifetime."

"I asked Mom the same question." Morgan stuffed her trash into her paper lunch sack and crushed it into a ball. "Anna says her uncle is out of town on a job with her father. It's just gonna be us."

Lucan's cheerful demeanor returned. "Then count me in." He shoveled the last two forkfuls of food into his mouth, chewed and swallowed quickly. "I'll walk you to class," he said, wiping his face with his napkin.

Lucan serviced his tray and they headed for the exit, dropping their paper trash into the garbage can on the way. A cold shiver ran down Morgan's spine. Feeling suddenly nauseous, she grabbed the hard edge of the plastic receptacle. The low growl of an animal echoed in a corner of her mind.

"Anything wrong?" Lucan steadied her by the shoulder.

Morgan looked around, but the cafeteria had faded into the background; the edges of her vision blurred. She felt the dark eyes watching her before she saw them.

An unkempt boy with long, scraggly black hair sat at an empty table in one corner of the lunch room. His deep brown eyes were bloodshot, his hands dirty. *This can't be right*, Morgan thought, wanting to look away but trapped in his gaze. *Doesn't anyone else see him?* She closed her eyes and willed her brain to clear. When she'd opened them again, the world had righted itself. The noisy chatter in the cafeteria rang in her ears.

She looked for the boy at the corner table, but the figure she saw sitting there looked nothing like her vision. In fact, he looked like any other guy. *Did I just imagine that?* Morgan rubbed her temple with one hand, clinging to Lucan's arm with the other. "Yeah, I'm fine," she told him. She scrutinized the kid as they passed, but didn't recognize him. He looked to be a little older than her, maybe a junior or senior. *Must be new to Molalla.*

The boy turned a serious face toward her. She shuddered. His brown eyes held her captive again, as if she were the only other person in the room. *Something's not right.* Morgan tried to shake it off a creepy feeling as she and Lucan left the building. *Not my problem*, she told herself. Morgan was determined to enjoy her first year in high school, and that meant no more strays needing help, and no more mysteries demanding to be solved.

* * * *

"Get ready." Mom was standing at the pen door, ready to open it. "Anything can happen."

Morgan shaded her eyes from the late afternoon sun and looked around the large yard, noting every obstacle between the enclosure and the tree farm beyond that made the Wildling home a perfect release site for deer. A manger full of hay and a tub of water served the local wild herd that would be the orphaned fawns' new extended family.

Anna, Mrs. Wildling, and Lucan had spread themselves an even distance from the enclosure, waiting for Morgan's mother to open the door. Four hand-raised deer with fading white spots paced the tall, ranch wire fencing of their corral. They had grown up in the protection of the paddock through the summer. Now it was time to introduce them to the world.

Morgan tried to distinguish the fawn found at the high school track from the others, but the dog bites had healed, the sutures had dissolved, and the fur had grown back to cover any scar. She couldn't tell it from the other orphaned fawns that had also been brought to the Wildlings for hand-raising over the last several months.

Mom unsnapped the latch, gently opened the gate, and took a quiet step back. Large ears swiveled to take in any sounds. Heads turned cautiously. The deer licked their noses and flashed their tails nervously before one of them dared to take its first cautious step. It was closely followed by the others until all four stood just outside the paddock.

One of the fawns stepped on a twig and it cracked loudly. It may as well have been an explosion. The deer jumped more than four feet off the ground as each bounded blindly in a different direction. A minute later, they halted and tensed again.

"Look," said Anna, mistaking the animals' panic for excitement. "They're happy to be free."

Another explosion erupted as her voice pierced the eerie silence. *Splash.* One of the deer tripped over the water tub and landed in it face first. *Bang. Scrape. Bang. Bang.* It struggled to get out.

Morgan sucked in her breath. "They're terrified."

Closest to the water container, Morgan reached for the deer to steady it and help it step out of the barrel. She tried to control her own panic, and sent the fawn mental messages of calm. Dripping wet, the frightened animal stood next to her for a few minutes before it took a few tentative steps and looked around for its friends.

Morgan's mom threw her a stern look. The deer was now too big to lift, and strong enough to be dangerous if it had kicked her. Helping it out of the tub had been a risk.

Leaves clattered from a bush nearby as the smallest of the four fawns struggled to free itself in from a tangle of branches. Unable to do so, it hung there suspended, panting from exertion.

Morgan watched her mom keep her body between the frantic animals and the ranch wire of their pen. If one of the fawns hit and slid down the fence it could easily catch and break a leg.

"Nobody moves," Mom ordered.

Anna's face was solemn now that she realized the precariousness of the situation. Everyone stood still and, as if taking their cue from their human caregivers, the deer calmed and started to seek out their siblings. They moved closer, instinctively drawing courage from one another.

"Should I untangle that one?" Lucan's voice was barely above a whisper as he nodded in the direction of the bush ensnared deer.

"No. It looks like it can get out of its own mess," said Mom. "Eventually."

Everyone breathed a sigh of relief when the young deer started to explore the yard, even nibble on grass and hay. "What happens now?" asked Mrs. Wildling.

"They'll stay in the protection of the yard," Mom told her as she led the way back toward the house. "You'll be able to support them until they venture off and join the wild herd. The fawns will learn what they need to from the group."

"Ouch." Morgan stuffed a purple-stained finger into her mouth. "I love blackberries," she said, "but not the thorns." She and Lucan had stayed to pick berries from the woods that bordered the Wildling house. Anna and her mother had retired to their home. Mom wouldn't be back to pick them up for at least a couple more hours. Morgan usually found gathering berries tedious, but she could pick for hours when she was with Lucan. *Even the worst job is easier when you have someone to do it with.*

"Blackberry pies are my favorite." Lucan's bucket was almost as full as Morgan's.

"The animals love berries too," said Morgan. "What we don't use for pies we freeze for feed through the winter." It was getting dark and she could feel the quiet of sunset, the in-between time before the day animals retired and the night animals ventured out. From where they were, she and Lucan could watch the fawns explore the Wildling yard. Morgan smiled and pointed to the smallest one, who'd finally managed to free itself from its bushy snare.

Morgan heard rustling nearby. A wild doe followed by a fawn about the same age as the four they'd just released stepped out of the forest and into the open. The deer took a few tentative steps toward the manger. She eyed the young deer warily, sniffing and listening for trouble.

"She's probably wondering where their mothers are," Morgan whispered to Lucan. "Another female could hurt her own baby."

The four orphans turned dark eyes toward the wild pair. None of them moved as they watched the adult deer walk cautiously to the hay.

"Will they eventually be adopted by wild mamas?" asked Lucan.

"Not usually. They'll follow them, live around them, and learn from them, but they'll always be outsiders." Morgan wished it could be different, but nature protects its own. She knew any efforts spent on raising another animal's offspring decreased the chances of your own surviving. It was a hard fact of life in the wild.

It wasn't long before other deer joined the doe and her fawn at the feeding trough. Though out-of-spots and wearing the gray-brown coat of an adult, these deer looked younger.

"Those are probably yearlings," said Morgan. "They don't have their own offspring yet."

The four wildlife center fawns kept a healthy distance.

"Will they hurt our babies?" asked Lucan.

"They could," Morgan admitted, "but we haven't found that to be a problem as long as there's plenty of food available. That's why we do these *soft* releases."

They watched the animals move freely around the yard.

"They don't seem scared of people," said Lucan.

"No," said Morgan. "Just of everything they don't know." *Which is a lot.* "They walk the line between people and predators." Morgan explained. "Most humans have dogs to keep away cougar and coyotes, the primary natural killers of deer. But those same dogs can attack the deer, and they can get hit by a car. And then there are hunters. Deer migrate deep into the woods during hunting season in October."

She took Lucan's hand and they headed toward the house before it got too dark to see. Furry heads popped up as they turned to leave. A meteor raced across the sky as if in a hurry to get to who knows where. Morgan shivered. It was another omen of change.

Lucan squeezed her hand. "Make a wish."

Morgan took a last look at the four young deer and whispered a prayer of thanks for her own family and friends. She didn't need to wish for anything.

* * * * *

All year long our children have grown,
now is the time to reap what we have sown.
We fed and cleaned to give them a chance
to live in the wild, their lives to enhance.

Back to nature they will be returned,
a second chance from our work was earned.
But there is more work yet to come
because our job is never done.

We release them now at this time of year
for food is plentiful, though predators near.
We pray they thrive and live without strife,
keep the hunters away, get a good chance at life.

So on this day let us just rest
for next year again we must do our best.
Beneath the sun's fading light
we will have fun and in games unite.

Through the maze we ponder and walk,
the Fates count the time by the tick of the clock.
Every step we take reveals a new turn
as each day draws nigh something new we do learn.

Cloudless nights and sun-drenched days,
at the bright stars we now will gaze,
a glimpse of what we hope there to be,
and in the heavens what we might see.

> Mother Nature, I humbly ask
> what they need to learn, let them do it fast.
> Watch over them now, if just for a while
> protect them from harm, they are without guile.
>
> No matter how hard, we must say good-bye.
> Tonight in my bed I know I will cry.
> These creatures were born to roam and be free.
> This is the way it was meant to be.

"Ah, Mom," Morgan cringed after her mother finished reading. "I wrote that when I was just a kid." She glanced at Lucan, red-faced.

"I don't care if it's simplistic," her Mom smiled wistfully. "I like it."

The five of them—Mom, Aunt Jackie and Uncle Rick, Morgan and Lucan—were standing in a half-circle facing the Molalla River. It was the third week of September, and they were celebrating the autumn equinox with an early evening picnic.

"I like it too." Lucan squeezed Morgan's hand, sending a wave of warmth up her arm.

"Time to release the red-tailed hawk." Mom interrupted their all-to-brief moment, unlatching the door of the crate at her feet. She took a step back to give the confused bird some space.

The animal didn't move. After months of living in a pen while its broken wing healed, it took a minute or so to realize freedom was within reach. The hawk swiveled its head to stare at its captors. Apparently it wanted to make sure this wasn't a trick before it took its first tentative step outside the travel enclosure. One more step and it spread its wings, gently ascending currents of air across the water.

Morgan caught her breath. *No matter how many times I watch an animal get released,* she thought, *it never gets old.*

They watched the hawk soar straight and true across the river, landing in a big leaf maple tree. The bird's dark red-and-brown coloring stood out amid the yellow and gold of the changing autumn leaf color.

"There goes the last of the orphaned and injured animals for the year," Jackie sighed. Morgan knew she was both glad and sorry to see it go. It was the same every autumn.

They stood silent for a while, waiting to see what the bird would do. It surveyed the area, collecting its bearings before finally taking off and disappearing into the dense canopy of trees. Months of work vanished in less than five minutes.

"Anyone for a toast?" asked Jackie, leading the way to the picnic basket. She pulled out a bottle of sparkling grape juice.

Morgan finished her glass quickly. Her stomach growled; the bubbles in her drink only made it louder. "What?" she giggled, red-faced. "I'm hungry."

Lucan graciously ignored her mortified expression. "What's for dinner?"

"Hunter's stew." Jackie pulled a large camping pot out of their picnic basket and unsnapped the lid; a delicious aroma floated on the air.

Lucan inhaled deeply. "I don't know what hunter's stew is," he said, "but it sure smells good."

"It's a mix of cabbage, pork, sausage, bacon, and mushroom." Jackie stirred the brown stew with a generous ladle. "I just toss it into a crock pot."

Rick handed out bowls and spoons. "You didn't tell him the secret ingredient," he smirked conspiratorially, then winked at Lucan. "Beer."

Mom gave her brother-in-law a stern glare. "The beer cooks off," she told them. "It just adds flavor."

"Awwww." Lucan grinned with mock disappointment as he took a bowl from Jackie.

They ate the stew with cornbread followed by large slices of blackberry pie. When they couldn't eat another bite, they played charades until it started to get dark.

"We'd better pack up while we can still see," said Mom. She gave her daughter a soft smile tinged with... *sympathy?* She ignored Morgan's furrowed brow. "You guys might like some time alone. We'll pack up. Meet us at the car when you're ready, say fifteen minutes?"

What gives? Morgan was confused. She'd only been dating Lucan a few weeks and had never been allowed to be alone with him outside of school or work.

Lucan nodded and offered Morgan a hand-up. "Wanna go for a quick walk?"

"Sure." Morgan stood up and brushed herself off before taking his hand. She pushed aside any misgivings, just happy to be alone with Lucan. *Maybe Mom finally trusts me. It's not like we can do anything with them around.*

They didn't wander far. Trees and bushes hid them from the adults. Not much was said as they watched bats swooping across the river and back catching insects with uncanny acrobatics. Finally Lucan turned to face her. His expression was subdued. "I've got to tell you something," he said.

Morgan's heart pounded. The air felt thicker somehow, harder to breath.

"I have to leave Oregon." He gave her a moment to let the shock sink in, then took a deep breath before explaining. "My parents told me they're getting a divorce."

Morgan glanced down the path they'd just walked. She thought of her mother's sad smile. *They knew*, she realized. *That's why Mom let us be alone.* Morgan's mind was a jumble.

"So?" She didn't want to believe it. "Why does that mean you have to leave?"

His sad blue eyes searched her face. "I have to go with my mom to Colorado to live with my grandparents until we sort this out."

Morgan blinked dumbfounded, choking back a sob. *This can't be happening*, her mind cried. *After all we've been through to finally get together.* The past year raced through her brain—the thefts, the break-ins, the kidnapping, their plan, and catching the man behind it all. Mostly, she remembered the push-pull of doubt and faith in Lucan. "You're coming back, right?" she asked, but she already knew the answer. *They never come back.*

"I don't know." He shook his head. "Not for a while. They've already enrolled me in school there. And I think my mom's found a job."

A tear escaped and ran down Morgan's face. She swiped it away. "We'd better go," she said, and headed back up the trail.

Lucan lagged a few steps behind as they walked back to the car.

All Hallows Eve

Morgan slipped off her black and white infinity bracelet and hung it on their tabletop memory tree. It looked lonely dangling from the black wrought iron branches amid all the pictures of dead "ancestors," most of whom Morgan had never known. She fingered a few of the tiny frames with photos of her pets that had passed away. In her household Halloween and All Souls Day were celebrated as days to remember.

"Lucan's *not* dead." Lawren huffed and plunked her hands on her hips. "You're being morbid, don't you think?" She pulled the leather band off the tree and handed it back to her friend.

"Our relationship is," Morgan retorted. "Or it may as well be." The girls were ready to go trick-or-treating, and just waiting for it to get dark enough to start their venture around town. Morgan usually looked forward to Halloween. Her Grim Reaper costume allowed her to wear heavier clothing underneath against the chilling weather, plus it fit her gloomy mood this year.

Tiny Lawren was wearing an ice princess costume; snowflakes trimmed the pale blue dress. A thick white cape with a fur-lined hood would help keep her warm. Of course, the outfit only reminded Morgan of her date with Lucan.

It had been just over a month since Lucan's forced move to Colorado with his mother. Contacts between him and Morgan had been few and far between, and had proved totally awkward. Morgan shoved her billowing frosted gray-black sleeve up, and put the leather band back on her wrist. Their long distance relationship was quickly shriveling away.

"We'll pray for your dying relationship tomorrow," Lawren scoffed. "Tonight we're going to enjoy Halloween."

"Have fun." Mom was cheerful as she handed each of them a plastic pumpkin basket to collect their candy. Morgan's was the traditional orange, but Lawren had painted hers icy-white to match her costume. Mom grabbed her car keys to drive them into town and gazed at them wistfully. "You don't know how much longer you'll be doing this."

She says that every year, thought Morgan. *Teenagers go trick-or-treating all the time in Molalla. After all, it's not like there's much else to do.* The town catered to both younger and older children. Most of the youngsters, followed by their parents, were already finished by the time it got dark. Morgan had to admit, it would be embarrassing to say, "trick or treat" in front of a bunch of *little* kids.

Mom dropped them off in the police parking lot at the center of town. "Pick you up here at ten."

The girls met up with a bunch of their friends. She half expected to see Zane in the same skunk costume he'd worn at the May Day Masquerade, patched tail and all, but he and Paige had dressed as Bonnie and Clyde for the evening. Morgan was glad, not sure she could have stood being reminded of Lucan and his raccoon costume all night. Megan looked great in green medieval garb. Her new boyfriend Dirk dressed as Robin Hood, complete with bow and arrows. Thano looked like a werewolf with mange in a costume that had obviously seen much wear over the years. Morgan glanced at her best friend, but it seemed Lawren was over Thano. She was flirting with a new guy whose name eluded Morgan. She inhaled deeply and plastered on a smile. *Looks like I'm the only one with no one interesting tonight.*

The group started their candy hunt by calling on the small shops and business. It didn't take long for the boys to separate from the girls so they could talk sports. Morgan relaxed. Being in a group of chattering teenagers helped her to stop thinking about her absent boyfriend. Shopkeepers, dressed in costumes, stood in open doorways and deposited candy, pencils, markers, crayons, and stickers into bags and baskets held open by expectant kids with the appropriate password, "trick or treat." The dentist handed out toothbrushes, floss, and mouthwash. The feed store dropped dog and cat treats in their bags. Most of the storefronts were decorated. Windows were painted with pumpkins and scarecrows, ghosts and graveyards, fairies and goblins. The small town really did-up All Hallows Eve.

Finishing with the shopkeepers, the company of friends spiraled out to the homes and apartments that surrounded the small business district. In between houses Morgan pushed her oversized hood down around her shoulders so she could talk to her companions and better see where they were going. The homes and apartments were decorated a lot more sinister than downtown. Spider webs, Hollywood monsters, and gravestones warned trick-or-treaters to approach with caution. Horror music and artificial fog filled the front porches of several of the residences and spilled into front yards.

The denizens of Molalla loved Halloween. In a couple of hours Morgan's and Lawren's baskets were getting quite heavy. They fell behind to compare their loot. "We'll pick out what we want after church tomorrow," said Lawren, "then donate the rest to the meals-on-wheels program." Morgan grinned as she thought of the "goblins" she'd bribed as a kid, leaving excess candy to disappear from the front porch overnight.

Lawren ran to catch up with the others, but Morgan stalled when the hairs on the back of her neck rose with an eerie sensation. *Someone is watching me.* She scanned the area suspiciously, but the street was full of costumed kids running from house to house without concern, ignoring her as far as she could tell. Most were barely careful to watch the minimal street traffic. *Why would anyone be following us?* Morgan turned full circle, straining to see into the shadowy areas created by street and porch lights. The creepy feeling didn't go away.

Morgan took a deep breath and tried to shake it off. *Just my overactive imagination,* she told herself. She searched for her group, but realized she was at a four-way corner. *Which way did they go?* She strained to see down each of the long streets, but didn't see any of her friends — or anyone, in fact.

She looked up at the dark sky and prayed. "Dear God, let me get to where I'm supposed to be." The moon, hidden behind thick clouds, offered no direction. It started to drizzle. *Great.*

Morgan caught a glimpse of a werewolf heading toward a smaller apartment complex down the quietest of the four streets. The road was lined with large oak trees whose gnarly bare limbs cast long shadows. "Thano?" she called out. Anxious to catch up with her friends, she ran toward the old building as fast as her billowy costume would allow.

Why would they come down here? Morgan wondered when she finally stopped. Most of the apartment lights in the complex were turned off, indicating that the residents had no interest in Halloween or trick-or-treating. She spotted the werewolf again at the far end of the complex under one of the working street lights. "Thano." Morgan waved, but again the boy didn't seem to hear her. She resumed her chase, stopping only when she realized the functioning street lights in this neighborhood were fewer, and it was darker here than she was comfortable with.

Morgan turned another full circle, then caught her breath as a chill overtook her. *I think I made a mistake.* She pulled her cloak tighter. *I don't think that was Thano. And this isn't a great place to be.* She took a few steps back toward the busy street corner from which she'd come, but it suddenly seemed very far away. She passed one oak tree, then another, on her way back. The hollows looked like eyes, the knots like noses. The branches rustled and limbs creaked in the growing wind.

I'm almost there. Morgan fixed her eyes on the lights ahead, forcing herself to breath while placing one foot in front of the other. *I'm not scared*, she assured herself. But then something grabbed her arm and pulled her into the shadow of one of the menacing trees. Morgan's back scraped against the rough bark as she was held by powerful hands. She stared into the dark bloodshot eyes of a feral monster. Morgan caught her breath, then blinked twice. *No. It's the guy from the cafeteria.*

"You've got to help me before I do something really bad," the boy pleaded. His scraggly black hair reached his shoulders as he stared up through the trees limbs. "The full moon is coming." A cloud moved over the shining orb, throwing the two of them into momentary darkness.

"Morgan, where are you?" Morgan heard Thano call out. When the cloud passed, the moonlight seemed brighter, more revealing. She saw Thano and Lawren heading her way.

"Over here," she yelled. The grip on her arms dropped away. Looking around, Morgan found herself alone; the boy had simply vanished.

"Where'd you go?" Lawren sounded relieved, and a little annoyed. "We were worried."

"Must've got lost." Morgan smiled sheepishly at her friends. "Gosh I'm glad to see you guys."

They headed back to the four-way corner. On the way Morgan searched the darkness, wondering how the boy had disappeared and where he might have gone. When she saw nothing, she turned her attention back to her friends and the holiday.

*As the wheel of the year goes round and round,
endings and beginnings are forever bound.*

The words echoed in Morgan's head as the boy's desperate plea for help played over and over in her mind. His face, his dark brown eyes, haunted her. She could feel another adventure coming like a cold breeze blowing in from the north; she wondered what surprises it might bring.

This is a work of fiction.

For true stories of the
American Wildlife Foundation
and the animals that live there,

check out our book
Whispers from the Wild,
at http://www.jajacquest.com

*Thank you for reading my book!
If you enjoyed it, please take a moment
to review it at your favorite retailer.*

Made in the USA
Middletown, DE
02 July 2015